She was *not* looking for Nick

Sydney leaned on the sill and craned her neck to watch the students and chaperones gathering in the street below. Nick exited the hotel and sauntered over to join the group. *Nick,* she hmphed. *Nick, Nick, Nick.*

He hadn't cast a single interested-male look in her direction since their chat in the cathedral. Which was fine with her. Really, truly fine. At least she hadn't been subjected to any more of those wolfish once-overs. Or that irritatingly smug charm.

Maybe he'd decided she wasn't worth the trouble. Maybe he didn't find her attractive enough, or interesting enough, or...

As if she cared. And she didn't. Not a bit. She had Henry to think about. Henry and his proposal. And whether she should accept it.

Or not.

Dear Reader,

One evening ten years ago, I placed my fingers on the computer keyboard and began to write something just for fun. Before that moment, I'd never written anything I didn't have to—no short stories, no poetry, no journal or diary entries—and I couldn't imagine what the results of my experiment might be. But a few hours later I'd produced a scene—a fictionalized account of something that had happened to me in Paris while I chaperoned a group of high school students on an educational tour.

You'll find that scene inside this book.

A Perfect Stranger is my first storytelling effort and a sentimental favorite. I enjoyed sifting through my memories of London and Paris to describe the settings, and I loved creating the characters and tossing them into all sorts of trouble. I hope you'll have as much fun reading this book as I had writing it.

I love to hear from my readers! Please come for a visit to my Web site or chat with me on my blog at www.terrymclaughlin.com. You can also find me at www.wetnoodleposse.com or www.superauthors.com. Or write to me at P.O. Box 5838, Eureka, CA 95502.

Wishing you happily-ever-after reading,

Terry McLaughlin

A PERFECT STRANGER
Terry McLaughlin

HARLEQUIN®

TORONTO • NEW YORK • LONDON
AMSTERDAM • PARIS • SYDNEY • HAMBURG
STOCKHOLM • ATHENS • TOKYO • MILAN • MADRID
PRAGUE • WARSAW • BUDAPEST • AUCKLAND

ISBN-13: 978-0-373-71467-4
ISBN-10:   0-373-71467-X

A PERFECT STRANGER

www.eHarlequin.com

Printed in U.S.A.

ABOUT THE AUTHOR

Terry McLaughlin spent a dozen years teaching a variety of subjects, including anthropology, music appreciation, English, drafting, drama and history, to a variety of students from kindergarten to college before she discovered romance novels and fell in love with love stories. When she's not reading and writing, she enjoys traveling and dreaming up house and garden improvement projects (although most of those dreams don't come true). Terry lives with her husband in Northern California on a tiny ranch in the redwoods. Visit her at www.terrymclaughlin.com.

Books by Terry McLaughlin

HARLEQUIN SUPERROMANCE

Don't miss any of our special offers. Write to us at the following address for information on our newest releases.

Harlequin Reader Service
U.S.: 3010 Walden Ave., P.O. Box 1325, Buffalo, NY 14269
Canadian: P.O. Box 609, Fort Erie, Ont. L2A 5X3

For Mom, a fellow tour survivor

CHAPTER ONE

SYDNEY GORDON stared at the engagement ring glittering in the candlelight and wondered what to say. What to do.

What to *feel*.

One thing she shouldn't be feeling was panic. No woman in her right mind would have this lung-squeezing, temple-throbbing reaction to a proposal from sweet, stable, handsome Henry Barlow, an attorney with a beautiful new home, a solid investment portfolio and an excellent chance of earning a partnership with a law firm in Truckee, California, before the end of the year.

Which meant she must be going crazy.

Even now the proof was bubbling through her, right along with the champagne in her nearly empty flute—those same fizzy, self-destructive impulses that had driven her from one disaster to another after her father had died four years ago and left her an unexpected insurance benefit and the means to go down in well-financed flames. Dropping out of her postgrad work in Education to dabble in Theater Arts. Leaping into an affair with an actor and dashing off to a regional Shakespeare festival. Playing an infamous seductress onstage and getting her heart stomped to pieces behind the scenes. Adding several more strands of gray to her mother's carefully coiffed hair. Getting duped, dumped, ditched, disillusioned and nearly disowned, though not necessarily in that order.

"Do you like it?" asked Henry.

"The ring?" Sydney gulped the rest of her champagne and gave him a brilliant smile. "It's beautiful. Absolutely *perfect*."

Henry would never disillusion her. Just look how carefully he'd staged this moment: the sunset view of Lake Tahoe from the restaurant window, the champagne tilting in an ice bucket, the jazz trio playing his sentimental request.

And that fabulous ring—the one-carat emerald-cut diamond with four baguettes set in a platinum band. She knew all this because Henry had just finished explaining it in great detail, along with a brief lecture on the importance of cut, clarity and something else she'd forgotten already.

She bit her lip, trying to remember. No good. Whatever he'd said, it was gone now.

"I'd like you to wear it while you're gone," he said.

"Gone?" She blinked. "Oh—the tour. Um…"

He reached for her hand, his grip as warm and steady as always. She hoped hers wouldn't seem clammy and limp by comparison.

"I'm going to miss you," he said.

"I'll only be in Europe a couple of weeks."

Two weeks—not much time to erase any lingering unease over those minor glitches during her substitute teaching stint and replace them with the image of an organized, responsible educator. Two weeks to chaperone a group of high school students on an early-summer tour through England and France, to make an excellent impression on the North Sierra school administration and secure that full-time position in the English department. To make a success of herself, at last.

Henry gave her fingers a gentle squeeze, and she realized she'd been drifting. She smiled again and reminded herself to be grateful she'd found a man like this, a man who cared enough to arrange every detail of this romantic setting. A man who would help her smother her impulses to be…well, impulsive.

There certainly was nothing impulsive about Henry. Witness his smooth wind-up: a minor adjustment of his stylish silk tie, that perfectly confident smile as he refilled her flute with champagne. Henry was so…so…

Perfect.

Not that perfection was a problem. Her mother, for instance, approved of Henry and reminded Sydney of that fact repeatedly—when she wasn't reminding Sydney of her rapidly approaching thirtieth birthday. Lately her mother was fixated on the concept that

Sydney's birthday, Henry's suitability and the state of matrimony were in some sort of cosmic alignment.

Poor Meredith Gordon. Sydney's mother had spent most of her adult life bandaging the family financial situation after each of her husband's inventions and subsequent development schemes had drained away most of their savings. She probably viewed Henry as the perfect match for a daughter who seemed to display a tendency to follow her father's eccentric, erratic example.

No, the problem wasn't Henry's perfection. The problem was that Henry was...well, that he...the thing was, Henry was so...

Persistent.

That was it: he was persistent. And lately his persistence about setting a wedding date had been scraping at her ambivalence like fingernails on a chalkboard. She glanced down at the fingers of the hand Henry wasn't holding as they drummed on the linen, and she curled them into a silent, polite fist.

However, Henry's persistence could be considered an admirable quality, even one point in his favor. She snatched up her wine to take another sip, relieved to have found something to stick in Henry's plus column.

Point two: timing. Henry's was excellent. Look how cleverly he'd timed this proposal for the evening before she left on the tour. And it was sweet of him to give her this ring to wear so she'd think of him while she was thousands of miles away.

Now, if she could just round up a few more items for her Reasons To Marry Henry list before he finished his lecture—er, his proposal…

The proposal. Oh, dear. Drifting again. She'd almost missed his pitch: perfectly beautiful words spilling from perfectly bowed lips above a perfectly square jaw. She smiled so hard, appreciating him so much that one of her eyes began to twitch.

They'd discussed marriage before, but never with anything approaching this degree of formality. Of finality.

Of inevitability.

And it was inevitable that she'd say yes, of course. Marrying Henry made perfect sense. They comple-mented each other surprisingly well—a perfect match, in so many ways.

The spasm in her eyelid intensified, and she hoped Henry couldn't see it and guess at the panic-driven insanity bubbling up inside her.

No, no, she told herself as she struggled with her ambivalence. *No, no,* she thought as she held her breath to strangle a particularly sneaky and senseless impulse, right up until the moment she opened her mouth and, riding a gust of pent-up air, out popped the one word neither of them wanted to hear: *"No."*

"No?"

"No! I mean…not *no.*" Sydney jabbed a finger against the corner of her eye and tried to shovel her way out of the muck of her latest impulse. "What I mean is…"

Henry gave her hand a comforting pat before

withdrawing his. "That's okay. You don't have to tell me what you mean."

"I don't?"

"We both know what we want," he said. "That's all that matters."

"You're right." She sighed with relief. Henry was nearly always right.

He snapped the lid over the ring and slid the little velvet box back into his pocket. "This will be here waiting for you when you get back," he said with a reassuring smile. "Just like me."

Sydney drained her second glass of champagne, coating one layer of fizziness with another.

At least the twitch was gone.

NICK MARTELLI leaned one shoulder against a limestone building in the Bloomsbury area of London and peered around the corner. A block away, an airport shuttle bus lumbered and shuddered to a stop in front of his hotel.

Using his crackerjack skills of observation, ace investigator Jack Brogan committed to memory every detail of the scene with one brief glance: the limousine gliding to a stop at the casino's entrance, the telltale bulge of a semiautomatic pistol in the doorman's uniform jacket, the silhouette of a gun barrel emerging from the inky gash of the nearby alleyway—

Nick narrowed his eyes as he considered which fictional character might be aiming the second gun and winced. He lifted a hand and gently tested a bruised and puffy cheekbone, a memento of his first—and last—stakeout with a private detective. There were safer, easier methods of researching story ideas for his novel-in-progress.

Methods like this trip to Europe.

He glanced at his watch. It was later than he'd realized—his brother had probably come in on an earlier shuttle and checked into the hotel. Joe was escorting half a dozen Philly high school students on a Tour of Two Cities, and Nick had offered to come along for the ride. Hanging out with Joe was one of his favorite things to do, and they hadn't shared an adventure for years.

He slipped his hands into his pockets and headed toward the hotel entrance, stopping at the corner to wait for a chance to cross. The shuttle driver stepped down, opened a compartment and unloaded luggage for the teenage tourists and tired-looking adults who streamed from the bus to collect it.

A few minutes later, one oversize case remained unclaimed on the sidewalk. The driver frowned at it, and then pulled a cigarette from his pocket and stepped behind the bus for a smoke.

The traffic signal changed, and the whooshing packs of taxis paused before him, but Nick stood staring at that case.

Jack recognized the driver who'd exited the midnight-black vehicle: a double agent he'd shadowed in Trieste, a man who'd snapped the neck of a friend at the order of a traitor, a man who would undoubtedly kill again without remorse. No passerby would have noticed the subtle signal that passed between the two men near the entrance, but Jack possessed an uncanny ability to detect the slightest subterfuge.

The agent opened the limo's rear door to extend a white-gloved hand to the vehicle's lone occupant. One long, slim, shapely leg ending in a stiletto heel slowly lowered to the curb, a siren-red sequined dress sliding tantalizingly up a shapely thigh. The mouthwatering thigh was attached to a drop-dead gorgeous blonde—

Make that a drop-dead gorgeous redhead.

No, a blonde.

Nick puckered his split lip and produced another wince instead of the soft whistle he'd intended. He hoped the drop-dead gorgeous strawberry-blonde who'd stumbled off the shuttle was a member of the Two Cities tour group.

She paused to shift the strap of a bulky purse higher on her shoulder and then whacked it against the side of the bus as she turned to retrieve a carry-on case on the step behind her. The bag caught on the shuttle's door, and she gave it a sharp tug. No use—stuck tight.

A frazzled female in need of assistance. An attractive female with ringless fingers. An opportunity for a casual introduction, which might be followed by any number of casual developments.

The traffic rolled to an idling halt again, and

Nick's lips twitched in a half grin as he stepped from the curb. His own powers of observation weren't too shabby, either.

SYDNEY SUCKED in a deep breath and tried again to pry her carry-on from the shuttle door. Her feet ached and her stomach growled, the hair that had sprung from its clip was either tickling the sides of her face or plastered to her forehead, and she suspected her deodorant had quit on the job somewhere over the Atlantic. Not that she wanted to check too closely.

Someone tapped her back, and she glanced over her shoulder at a shocking mess of a face, battered features twisting in some distorted, devilish version of a grin. Whatever the terrifying stranger said to her was drowned out in the blare of a passing car's horn, and all she could manage was a tiny squeak and a confused nod as she scrambled to process what was happening.

A mugging.

He reached past her to grip her case and unhook it from the door. She grabbed for the dangling zipper tag and yanked hard, trying to snatch it away. A tactical error. Toiletries and lingerie geysered up and rained down over the pavement of Tottenham Court Road.

He loomed over her intimate apparel, his shaggy black hair waving around his five-o'clock—no, forty-eight-hour shadow, the startling white of his crooked grin slashing through a deeply tanned complexion, and his dark eyes glinting with whatever muggers' eyes glinted with.

He certainly was a good-looking criminal specimen. But he was also eyeing the lacy pink bra draped over the curb. That made him either greedy, or a pervert, or both.

A greedy pervert with a slightly swollen purpled eye and a nasty gash in his upper lip. Someone had recently given him some trouble. And at that moment she was jet-lagged and caffeine-charged enough to want to give him some more, especially when he reached for her underwire with the front clasp.

"No!" she shouted as she leaped into action to rescue her bra. The strap on her shoulder slipped, and her hefty tote swung in an accidental but impressive arc. A thick London street guide, electronic organizer, tour paperwork, collapsible umbrella, camera, bottled water and the latest Dick Francis mystery novel connected with his jaw. It all made a satisfying *thwack*. He grunted and staggered, and then slipped on her black half slip and went down, hard.

"Help! Thief!" she yelled.

"Hey! Ms. Gordon!" Two of her students raced down the steps at the entrance of the Edwardian Hotel. The teenage boys skidded to a stop and stared, wide-eyed, at the stranger. "This is so, like, *whoa,* you know?" said Zack.

Sydney knelt to cram her bra back into the wreck of her carry-on. "I hit him with my purse."

"Cool!" said Matt. He pulled a video camera from his fanny pack. "Hit him again."

He aimed the camera at Sydney and then panned toward the lingerie littering the street. "Whoa. Edit."

Zack reached for the slip but snatched back his hand. "Hey, Ms. Gordon, I'd like to help you out here, but I don't think we should be touching this stuff, you know? Sort of messes with the student-teacher relationship."

The thief dabbed blood from his lip as the camera angled down for a close-up. "Get that thing out of my face," he growled.

Sydney froze at the sound of his gruff American accent. She peered more closely at the handsome man she'd knocked to the ground—a man who was making no effort to flee the scene of his foiled crime. Levi's jeans, Nike shoes, Philly Cheese Steak T-shirt. And a scowl registering annoyance rather than guilt.

Oh, dear. Maybe she'd overreacted, she considered with a familiar sinking feeling. Maybe he was a gentleman trying to assist her with her luggage. Not a thief.

Not a mugger.

Oh. My. God. Her cheeks torched up like road flares, and she stifled a mortified groan. *I'm the mugger.*

Her victim squinted at her through his swollen eye. "These kids belong to you?"

She nodded and swallowed a big gulp of guilt. "My students. Matt, Zack, this is…I'm sorry, I didn't catch your name."

She knew she should also introduce herself, but she wasn't sure of the proper etiquette following

assault and battery. Should the introductions come
before the apology, or after? Right now would be a
handy time to grovel, since she was already on her
knees. "I'm so, *so*—"

"'Help, thief' works for me." He stood and
slapped gutter grime off his jeans. "That's Mr. Thief
to you," he told the boys.

"I'm Sydney. Sydney Gordon. And I'm so, *so*
sorry about the misunderstanding." She got to her feet
and made a grab for her Bugs Bunny nightshirt, but
he beat her to it. "Thanks," she said, "but I can finish
this myself."

"Now I know why chivalry is dead. Women like
you keep knocking it on its ass." He shook out the
nightshirt and stared at Bugs. "I was only trying to
help you with your luggage."

"I just figured that out. And I really am *terribly*
sorry." She retrieved the shirt and stuffed it into her
case with shaky hands, averting her eyes and wishing
she could stuff herself down the nearest sewer
grate.

Before she could offer another apology, a balding,
rumpled version of Mr. Thief stepped through the
hotel entrance and ambled down the steps to join
them. He stopped behind the boys and watched her
knight in shining shiner pluck her butterfly print
panties from the bus fender.

"You're losing your touch, Nick," said the
stranger. "You don't usually have to work this hard
to get your hands on a woman's panties."

"She thought I was a thief." He ran a hand through

his thick hair and chuffed out an exasperated-sounding breath. "Do I look like a freakin' thug?"

The newcomer studied the bruised face with a frown before shoving a wide hand at Sydney. "Hi. Joe Martelli. The criminal's brother."

His brother. She took his hand and pasted on a faint smile. "Sydney Gordon. How do you do?"

"I'm doing okay." He frowned at Nick. "Where have you been? The desk clerk said you checked in hours ago. And what happened to your eye?"

"I walked into a door."

"What about the lip?"

Nick flicked a glance at Sydney. "It was a double door."

Time for another abject apology. "Nick, I—"

He cut her off with the wave of a hand and glanced at the boys. "Looks like Ms. Gordon has her stuff about ready to go now. Can you guys help her carry it in from here?"

Matt shoved his camera back into his fanny pack and slipped his fingers through the handle of her big suitcase. "Yeah. It's cool."

"Thank you, Matt," said Sydney before turning to face the Martellis. "It was nice meeting you. Both of you."

Joe grinned. "You, too."

"Yeah." Nick's grin widened but ended on a wince. "Nice."

Sydney winced, too, and then turned to flee the scene of her crime.

CHAPTER TWO

TWO DAYS SINCE botching her response to Henry's proposal, two hours after jolting into Heathrow, two steps from escaping the crowded shuttle, and she'd decked the first person she'd met in London. As a chaperone, she was setting a lousy example for her students.

But why waste daylight hours wallowing in the latest disaster? There were bound to be plenty of sleepless nights ahead for instant replays of her most embarrassing moments. Right now she should be cataloging her impressions of London as she followed Matt and Zack through the hotel entrance: clipped boxwood in planters, beveled glass in leaded panes, Etonian accents and hints of lemon oil and lavender in the air. She paused to absorb the English atmosphere through her pores.

I'm here, she thought for the umpteenth time since the jet had skidded onto European soil, and the thrill shivered through her, quicksilver and ice. *I'm really here.*

Sydney took a deep breath and brushed at the sticky bangs on her forehead. Time to get her act together. She had to ace this chaperoning gig. Her recent stint as a long-term sub hadn't provided her with many chances to showcase her talents for thorough preparation and making the most of every educational possibility.

Talents she'd be working her tail off developing during the next two weeks.

"Syd!" Gracie Drew, fellow faculty member and tour roommate, waved to her from the reception counter. Gracie's fuchsia-and-lime Hawaiian-print shirt glowed like a neon abstract in the crowd of teens and chaperones. "Hey, Syd. What took you so long?"

"You don't want to know." She pulled the strap of her weighty tote from her shoulder with a sigh. "But I'm here now. And ready to collapse in our room."

"Better keep the meltdown to a minimum," said Gracie, handing her a room key. "Heard we've got a meeting with the tour director in the Palladian Lounge in twenty minutes."

Matt and Zack dumped Sydney's luggage at her feet and turned to melt into the crowd.

"Hold it, fellas," she said in her official chaperone voice. "Where do you think you're going?"

Zack shrugged. "I dunno."

"How about your room?" Gracie pulled a stick of Juicy Fruit from its foil pack and folded it into her mouth. "Ms. Gordon and I'll come around to check on things in a while."

The boys headed toward the elevator, and Sydney sighed and shoved wavy bangs from her eyes. "Hope we can get everyone fed and settled early tonight. The tour company packed the itinerary pretty full tomorrow."

"Guess they figure they're going to cram some culture into these kids or die trying. Good thing they're giving us a couple of free afternoons to— *hey.*"

Gracie smiled and beckoned to someone behind Sydney. "Here's another teacher I want you to meet. Great guy. You'll love him. From Philadelphia. Came in with one of the groups on the earlier shuttle. Joe, come and meet Sydney."

Sydney figured it was pointless to hope that Gracie's acquaintance wasn't the same Joe who had already seen her underwear. She gritted her teeth to keep a smile in place and turned to find both Martellis staring at her, hands tucked into pockets and wearing matching slouches.

"Hi, Sydney," said Joe. "Small world, isn't it?"

"And this must be Nick." Gracie took his hand and gave it a quick, hard pump as she stared at his face. "Looks like you ran into some trouble."

"Not me," said Nick. "I ran away as fast as I could."

"Smart move." She smiled. "I'm Gracie Drew, North Sierra High. That's near Tahoe, on the California side."

"Glad to meet you, Gracie."

Nick cocked his head to one side and stared at Sydney for several long, loaded moments. "Hello, Sydney."

Her smile stretched to the snapping point.

"Well…" Joe rocked back on his heels. "Looks like we're all going to be spending lots and lots of time together. One big, happy family. I don't know about the rest of you, but I'm looking forward to it."

"May I help you carry your things to your room?" Nick asked Sydney.

"Thank you, but it's really not necessary."

"Oh, but I insist," he said. "It's the chivalrous thing to do."

He grabbed her suitcase handles and headed toward the elevator, snaking through the crush as she followed in his wake. He stopped and pushed the button, and then leaned down to murmur in her ear. "Maybe we could meet for dinner tonight. I could dump your plate in your lap, and you could toss my drink in my face. For old times' sake."

"Sounds delightful." She ignored the way the throaty rumble of his voice seemed to vibrate along her spine. "Maybe some other time."

"Okay," said Nick. "'Some other time' works for me." And then he flashed his subtle, crooked smile, and his dark eyes glinted with something that may not have been muggerish but assaulted Sydney's nervous system all the same.

Oh, dear.

NICK EDGED HIS WAY through scattered clumps of tourists at noon two days later, aiming for the rim of St. James Park facing the gates of Buckingham Palace. He wasn't looking for a different perspective on the Changing of the Guard; he was looking for a patch of grass suitable for a nap. He selected an empty space, stretched out on his back, linked his hands behind his head and closed his eyes.

A guard officer shouted a fresh set of commands, and the band struck up another rousing number. Horses' shoes clopped along the pavement in counterpoint to clicking cameras. British sunshine bathed his beaten face and soothed his fading bruises with politely reserved warmth.

What an idiot he'd been to volunteer for that stakeout. Instead of gaining a first-person perspective on surveillance techniques, he'd proved he had no talent for investigation and served himself up as a punching bag for a frustrated philanderer.

He'd thought these weeks in Europe would be a less painful source of story ideas, but once again he'd been driving on the wrong side of the brain. Here he was, helping his brother ride herd on a handful of culture-stunned teens, researching nothing more dangerous than some setting details, and he'd gotten clobbered by a paranoid with a mugger phobia.

Make that a very attractive paranoid muggerphobic.

The willowy blonde settled a bloodred nail over one of the buttons on her cell phone and pressed it a split second longer than necessary. Jack knew at once she'd sent a message to the network. He watched her tuck a hank of her long, wavy hair behind one delicate ear and drop the phone into her

*shiny black leather purse, an innocent-looking
courier's bag filled with the codes for—*

A soft-shelled shoe nudged Nick's ribs, and Joe's
voice floated down to him. "Aren't you worried
someone might step on you?"

Nick slitted one eye open and watched his brother
stuff the last of a shrimp-and-egg sandwich snagged
from a corner grocery into his mouth. Joe's breeding
showed: he was obviously the disheveled descen-
dant of some barbarian horde that had laid waste to
the countryside.

Nick settled his head back more comfortably into
his hands. "You're the only 'someone' I know who
could be that clumsy," he said.

"Not the only one."

"Ah, yes." Nick grinned. "Ms. Sydney Gordon.
Shiva, The Destroyer."

"Poor kid." Joe wadded the paper wrapper and
crammed it into a litter-loaded pants pocket. "That
pamphlet display was an accident waiting to happen.
Probably wasn't attached to the wall right or something."

"Yeah. Got to watch out for that steel-bolts-and-
stone combo." Nick shut his eyes. "And just think of
the hundreds of early-morning commuters she saved
from getting mangled in a faulty turnstile."

"Those little tube ticket slots are kind of tricky."

Nick snorted and crossed one ankle over the other.
One more mystery to unravel: Why was that California teacher wound so tight? She spent every waking
moment fussing over the tour, the time, the transpor-

tation, the weather, her kids and, for all he knew, this week's market levels of imported Danish herring. It was enough to make a guy wonder if ulcers could be contagious.

On the other hand, something about her was sparking story ideas so fast he could barely jot them down before they shimmied and morphed into others. She was definitely…stimulating.

The band shifted tempo and the guards' boots stomped to a new processional beat. Joe poked again with his sports shoe. "Don't you want to watch?"

"I did watch. Can't see much more than the backs of tourists and the tops of those furry black hats."

"Did you see Edward anywhere?"

"First plaid umbrella on the right." Nick's lips twitched at the thought of their *GQ* tour director. "Moving out fast, now that he's off the clock. Probably headed to the tour guide pit stop to get the circulation pumped back into his arm. I don't see how he can hold that thing up in the air all day."

"Stiff upper arm, old chap," said Joe in some kind of accent that might have been John Wayne channeling Henry Higgins.

"That's lip."

"Huh?"

"Lip," said Nick. "Stiff upper lip."

"Speaking of upper lips…"

Nick groaned. "Not again."

"Was it a bar brawl?" asked Joe. "You could tell me if you got beat up in a bar brawl, right? Especially the details."

"It wasn't a bar brawl."

"You'd tell me if it was, though, right?"

"Yeah, I'd tell you."

"So...it wasn't a bar brawl."

Nick opened one eye and stared at his brother. "It wasn't a bar brawl."

"Okay," said Joe with a shrug, looking disappointed. "Just asking."

Another limo eased by, ferrying another overdressed group out of an ornate palace gate. The crowd of tourists began to thin as the festivities dragged past the half hour mark.

"Where are we taking the kids after this?" Joe asked. "We're on our own for lunch and sightseeing this afternoon."

"You're the one with the itinerary and the responsibilities." Nick sat up and dangled his wrists over his knees. "I'm just along for the ride."

"You keep saying that."

"Because it's true," said Nick. "Your job. Your students. I'm not the one with the teaching credential."

"But you're the scheduling whiz."

"Not anymore."

No more bidding anxiety, no more site hassles, no more delivery migraines, no more deadline insomnia. No more specialty contracting business, now that he'd shut it down for the yearly hiatus. And no more weekly hassles with his house renovation cable television series, now that he'd passed most of the hosting duties to an assistant and assigned himself a consulting spot. Life was too short to live it in a state of perpetual stress, especially when he had enough money in the bank to take a nice, long break.

He had an eye for the possibilities in a project and a knack for building, the skills to pull a project together and an ease before the camera that played well on the small screen. But he had other talents to develop, other dreams to pursue.

Becoming a bestselling novelist, for instance. He wanted more than anything to see his name on something other than short pieces in pulp magazines.

"I'm retired," he reminded Joe. "And staying that way."

"You say that every year." Joe shifted his backpack over his shoulder and wiped his hands on his pants. "Guess I could go ask Sydney what she's planning. I think she's still over there, next to the fat lady's foot."

Only Joe could dismiss the statue of Queen Victoria, Empress of All She Surveyed—including the elegant stretch of The Mall—as "the fat lady."

Nick stood and scanned the tourists clumped around the base of the Victoria Memorial, looking for another statuesque lady—one with long, reddish-gold hair tucked up under a silly straw hat. "Good idea," he said. "She's probably got the tour schedule tattooed on her wrist, underneath a watch that tells the time in ten foreign capitals and the research headquarters in Antarctica."

"She's not that bad."

"You're right," said Nick. "She's worse."

"She just likes to be organized. At least she's paying attention."

"She takes notes on Edward's jokes, for cryin' out loud."

"Admit it," said Joe. "You're attracted to her."

Nick spied the lady in question and shrugged at the obvious: willowy build, interesting curves, Nicole Kidman coloring. He wished it were as easy to shrug off the less obvious *something* about her that kept registering on his radar, but that was a much tougher trick. "What's not to be attracted to?"

"Ha," said Joe. "I knew it."

While they watched, something that looked like a city map and a fistful of tube tickets spilled out of Sydney's oversize tote and fluttered to the pavement. She didn't seem to notice.

"Damn," said Nick.

CHAPTER THREE

NICK STARED AT Sydney's things littering the ground, and he knew he should go over there and help her out. But he froze in place, letting his overwhelming urge toward chivalry duke it out with an eerie sense of déjà vu—not to mention the instinct for self-preservation.

"Better go pick that stuff up," said Joe as he hitched his backpack higher on his shoulder. "She might not realize she dropped it."

"No way," said Nick. "If I kneel near her feet, she'll think I'm trying to look up her skirt, and she'll flatten me with that weapon of mass destruction she carries over her shoulder. I don't want another concussion."

Joe glanced at Nick's black eye with a frown. "Another one?"

"Aren't those some of your girls mixed in with the California group?" asked Nick, hoping to distract him. "Go grab 'em. I'll round up the boys."

Joe caught his arm before he could make an escape. "Don't forget, you promised you'd share lunch duty this afternoon."

"Yeah." Nick shoved his hands into his pockets

and shot a wry grin at his brother. In theory, this trip was supposed to be a chance to escape the extended Martelli clan and spend some rare one-on-one time with Joe. In practice, it came with forty-two fellow tour members attached at the hip. "I did."

They crossed to the island when the traffic slowed, and Nick helped Joe herd his scattered students toward the statue's base. Gracie's construction-cone-orange shirt was as easy to spot as Edward's umbrella.

"Greetings, Martellis," she said with a smile that quirked up around the wad of gum in her cheek. "Looks like we're the last of the group. The Albuquerque and Chicago folks already left for the London Eye."

"We were just discussing our plans for this afternoon," said Sydney.

"Figures," said Nick. He ignored the slitted look she shot him and pointed behind her. "You dropped something. Again."

She treated him to one of her nose-in-the-air looks before she bent to collect her things. God, she was cute when she was annoyed. Maybe that's why he kept poking at her. Immature, maybe, but a fellow had to play to his strengths.

"Where are you going?" asked Joe.

"We were getting ready to flip a coin," said Gracie. "Heads, Harrods. Tails, anywhere else."

"Heard there are some great food stalls at Harrods," said Joe.

Nick sighed and shook his head.

Sydney stood and wedged her papers back into her purse. "Maybe we should think of something a little more educational."

"Educational?" Gracie chewed over the suggestion with a frown.

"Exactly." Sydney fussed with the strap on her shoulder. "There are plenty of museums—"

"And we're gonna see 'em all," said one of the North Sierra boys. He scowled and scuffed his toe against a marble step.

Museums. Shopping. Not exactly the typical male teen's plan for a sunny afternoon in a foreign country.

Nick turned to Sydney with his most ingratiating smile, the one he'd perfected for dealing with rabid materials suppliers. "You know," he said, "there's a museum right down the street from Harrods."

"Yes." Her brows drew together above a suspicious frown. "The Victoria and Albert."

"What about lunch?" asked Joe. "Those food stalls sounded pretty good."

Nick kept his eyes locked on Sydney's. "Maybe we can work out a deal here."

"What kind of a deal?" asked Gracie.

"You and Joe and Sydney can take the shoppers to Harrods. And the food stalls," he added with a pointed glance at his brother. "I'll take the 'anywhere else' crowd."

"To the museum?" Sydney asked.

"Yeah," said Nick, "we'll head that way."

She produced one of the guidebooks she seemed to have sewn into the lining of her clothes and checked the Victoria and Albert's admission policies and closing times, food service and rest rooms, gift shop and special displays. She noted tube lines and transfers, currency exchange opportunities, the location of the American embassy, the nearest medical facility and the precise time Nick was to return to the hotel with the students. She handed him a card with her cell phone number and jotted his on the back of another.

He let her lecture break over him like a wave and tried to figure out what was sucking at him in the undertow. Maybe it was the way her feathery eyebrows puckered in concentration, or the way one slightly crooked front tooth gnawed at her plump lower lip. Maybe it was the scent of peachy shampoo and warm woman tickling his nose. Whatever it was, it made him wonder whether she was wearing those tiny butterfly panties.

Gracie cut the lecture short, deputized him as an official chaperone and led Sydney, Joe and their students off toward Birdcage Walk. Nick struck out across the square in the other direction. The three North Sierra boys who'd decided to take their chances with him jogged to catch up.

"Are we really going to some dumb museum?" one of them asked.

"No," said Nick.

"I thought you told Ms. Gordon that's where we were going."

"I told her we'd head that way." He grinned at the boys. "I didn't say we'd go inside."

SYDNEY PACED the wide, fanlit entry to the dining room of the Edwardian Hotel that evening, staging a murder. She pictured the set design and costuming, imagined the sound effects and lighting. The blast of a pistol—no, the flash of a knife. "Yes," she muttered. "A knife."

She flicked her wrist and frowned at her watch. Two minutes since she'd last called Nick Martelli's cell phone and listened to his gruff voice tell her to leave a message. Five minutes until the dinner scheduled for the tour group. An hour past the time Nick had promised to return with her students.

"A big, fat butcher knife," she muttered.

The cheery *bing* from the nearby elevator heralded Gracie's arrival. She'd traded her tire-tread touring sandals for evening footwear: sequined flip-flops. "Are they back yet?" she asked.

Sydney shook her head. "Haven't seen them down here."

"Nick'll bring them back any minute, safe and sound."

"But they were supposed to check in over an hour ago." She snuck another useless glance at her watch. "And we're leaving for the theater shortly after dinner. What if something awful happened?"

"You know what, Syd?" Gracie gave Sydney's cheek a motherly pat. "You worry too much. In between chaperoning duties, you should find some space to appreciate this experience yourself, don't you think?"

"You're right." She took a deep breath and battled back another queasy ripple of panic. "And everything so far has been wonderful. I still can't believe I'm finally here."

"Me, neither," said Gracie. "Not after I saw your packing lists."

Sydney shifted to let a few members of the tour group pass into the dining room. "Organization is important."

"Important, yes. A religion, no."

"You're right. I guess I should loosen up." A bit. Organization was a handy tool for maintaining control—not to mention a method for keeping impulses in check. "I just want to make sure that everything goes as smoothly as possible," she said.

Gracie slipped the neon-pink Princess Diana bag from her shoulder and fiddled with the strap buckle. "I still don't know why you think you need this chaperoning gig to clinch that full-time teaching spot. You already did a bang-up job as a long-term sub."

Sydney winced at the term *bang-up*. It brought back images of the fiasco of a spring play her drama class had unleashed on the public—exploding props, disintegrating scenery. "Thanks. But I—"

"Things'll go the way they're going to go, with or without you micromanaging the details."

"You're right." Sydney sighed. "Sorry."

"I haven't lost a student yet on one of these Europe jaunts. They're probably just having an adventure and lost track of the time. Nick'll take care of them."

Gracie's face went soft and dreamy. "That man's one in a million. And the kids love him."

"Nick, Nick, Nick." Sydney rolled her eyes. "What is it about that guy that turns everyone to mush?"

"Incredible charm? A great sense of humor?" Gracie tugged the purse strap through the buckle. "And the rear view isn't too shabby, either."

"Gracie!"

"Hey, just because I'm married and closing in on middle age doesn't mean I'm blind. And I'm not the only one indulging in figure appreciation. It's obvious that Nick admires yours."

Sydney ignored the tiny buzz of feminine satisfaction and reminded herself to be offended. "Just how obvious?"

"Enough to be flattered. Not enough to duck behind the nearest potted palm." Gracie lifted the shortened purse strap over her shoulder. "Climb out of the greenery, girl. Give the guy a little encouragement."

"Even if I wanted to flirt back—and I definitely don't," said Sydney, "this isn't the time or the place. I don't think indulging in a flirtation would set a very good example for the students."

"Hmm. Thirty hormonal teens spying on every move. I can see where that might put a damper on things." Gracie frowned. "Speaking of romantic challenges, Mr. Nine Lives called a few minutes ago."

"Henry?"

Yes, Sydney reminded herself, *Henry*. The man who should have been the number one reason to dive into the greenery and avoid mush-inducing Nick Martelli. The fact that Henry hadn't been the number one consideration was turning out to be problem number two. "Henry called here?"

"Yeah, he did. He sounded pretty disappointed he'd missed you, too. And he asked me to give you a message. I'd rather not, if you don't mind, since I'm about to sit down to dinner and I don't want to spoil my appetite."

"Sorry," said Sydney with an apologetic smile. "He's just being sweet."

"Sweet enough to make my teeth ache." Gracie shook her head. "What's up with that guy, anyway?"

"What do you mean?"

"Any man who keeps hinting about marriage the way he does should either cough up a ring or cut you loose to find someone else who will."

Sydney shifted uncomfortably. "He did."

"He cut you loose?"

"He proposed."

Gracie's gaze cut to Sydney's left hand. "I don't see a ring."

"That's because I didn't take it." Sydney lifted her ringless left hand and made a show of checking the time. "Nick is now officially late."

Gracie clamped her hand over Sydney's watch and shoved her arm back to her side. "What was wrong with the ring?"

"Nothing."

"Then what's wrong with him? Besides the obvious."

"Nothing," said Sydney with an exasperated sigh. She couldn't understand Gracie's disapproval. Henry had never been anything but flawlessy polite to all her friends. "There's *nothing* wrong with him."

And these days in Europe would help emphasize that fact. Absence made the heart grow fonder, after all. She was certain she'd gain a fresh perspective on the situation and renew her appreciation for all of his wonderful qualities. He was perfect husband material, after all. "He's not what you think. He's…"

She paused, waiting for inspiration. It didn't strike. "He's a very nice man."

Gracie snorted. "Faint praise if ever I heard it."

"And punctual." Sydney watched white-jacketed waiters ferrying dinner plates from the kitchen. Henry would never keep her waiting and wondering.

Here was one of those fresh perspectives she'd been hoping for. Compared to Nick Martelli, Henry looked absolutely…

Perfect.

Adolescent voices and the shuffle of oversize feet echoed from around the corner. Sydney sagged with relief. "Here come the boys."

"Well, well, well." Gracie waved the latecomers toward the dining room. "Have a few tales to tell?"

"The best, Mrs. Drew." Zack grinned. "We were in a riot."

Sydney gasped. "A riot?"

"A rally, not a riot," Eric said. "Nick took us over to watch some sheiks demonstrating."

"Sikhs," corrected Matt. "Sikh separatists, at the Indian embassy.

"But first we stopped for drinks in a pub," added Eric.

"What?" A big, fat, *dull* butcher's knife.

"We only had sodas. Nick had that brown stuff."

"Ale," Zack added. "It was gross."

Sydney's eyes narrowed. "And how do you know that?"

"He let us each have a taste." Zack cast an uneasy glance at the others. "Nick says it's important to experience other cultures."

"I'll have to ask Mr. Martelli all about it," she ground out. "He certainly has some interesting ideas about educational tours."

"I'll tell you all about our afternoon, Ms. Gordon," rumbled a familiar voice from just behind her shoulder. "And even toss in an apology or two, if you'll join me for dinner."

She turned to face Nick Martelli. He gazed down at her, his deep-set eyes glittering like obsidian. Impudently they surveyed the scooped neckline of her chambray dress.

Sydney clenched her toes inside her sandals, miffed at the frank appraisal of his gaze and the automatic tingle of her reaction. Then she straightened her backbone and lifted her chin. She refused to become just another serving of mush. "Welcome back, Mr. Martelli. I wasn't sure you were going to make it."

"Nick. The only 'Mr. Martelli' here is my brother." He slipped a broad palm around her arm. "Now, how about dinner?"

"Oh, but I—Mrs. Drew and I—"

"Go ahead," said Gracie with a wave. "The boys can fill me in."

Nick's fingers closed to form a polite manacle.

Neatly trapped. With her control of the situation slipping, Sydney gritted her teeth in what she hoped would pass for a smile. "All right, then. I wouldn't want to cause any trouble."

"No trouble, Ms. Gordon." Nick's grin spread in a dazzlingly innocent smile. "No trouble at all."

CHAPTER FOUR

NICK WASN'T QUITE sure why he'd blurted out that dinner invitation. Must have been the challenge in Syd's snotty tone and mulish expression—or the temptation of her plump, pouty lower lip. Nearly made a guy want to keep her on edge and ready to nibble. And the escort move had given him an excuse to get his hands on her. One hand, anyway—on a soft, slender female arm.

Which was as far as he was likely to get. Apparently Ms. Gordon had a boyfriend. Nothing serious, according to the student spies he'd pumped for information this afternoon, but Syd's type rarely viewed a relationship with an eligible male as anything other than serious.

And that was too damn bad.

With a cunning, lightning-fast move—a move that came second nature to an expert in the martial arts—Jack pinned her to the wall. Her icy expression melted into a dangerously seductive pout and her hot breath scorched his lips. Her breasts heaved from the exertion of her useless battle against him, pressing against the onyx studs of his crisply starched shirt.

He led her toward the noisiest table in the room, where Joe sprawled at one end, calmly cramming a dinner roll into his mouth while his jostling students rattled the tableware and nearly overturned the water pitcher.

"You're back," said Joe as Nick pulled out a chair for Sydney. "There is a God."

"Would've been back sooner," said Nick, taking the seat next to hers, "but we were detained by the police."

Joe spared him a brief glance. "What happened this time?"

"*This* time?" The frost in Sydney's tone threatened to freeze-dry the pot roast on their plates.

"We witnessed a fender-bender," said Nick with a shrug. "The bobby on the scene probably could've done his job without our help, but you know how kids eat that stuff up. I let them take their time, enjoy their little moment of glory."

He filled Syd's water goblet and smoothly changed the subject. "Your students tell me you're an actress."

"Not really." One of her eyelids fluttered in what looked suspiciously like a nervous tic. "At least, not lately. Not professionally, anyway."

"But isn't that what you teach?" Nick asked. He motioned for a waiter to bring another bread basket. "Drama?"

"I'm not really a teacher, either," she said, dropping the aristocratic pose to shift in her chair. "Not regular full-time, anyway. I was subbing.

Drama in the afternoon. Mornings, a few English classes."

"And now you're doing this tour." Joe scooped up some mashed potato. "Not much time left for acting."

"Don't you miss it?" asked Nick. He stretched one arm along the back of her chair as he leaned in close to snag the saucer of butter pats. "The passion, the glamour? The applause?"

She flinched as his thumb brushed the back of her dress, and he dropped his arm. "Um, yes. And no."

"Meaning?"

"Meaning I still act occasionally. With a local community group." She poked at her salad. "But the jobs behind the scenes interest me more than any role I've played."

"What jobs?" asked Nick. "Why are they more interesting?"

"Nick." Joe shot him a warning frown. "Pass the salt. Please."

Nick shoved the shaker across the table and turned to face Sydney. There was something there—a troubling something that shadowed her blue eyes. Something mysterious. Something interesting. Something… "How did you get into acting?" he asked. "Did you study drama in college?"

Something shoe-like nudged his shin. "Please pass the pepper," said Joe. He took the container and set it next to the salt with a determined *clunk*. "Ignore the third degree, Ms. Gordon. It's a bad habit."

"I'm a writer," said Nick.

"He's a pest," said Joe.

Syd smiled uncertainly and forked up a bit of limp lettuce. When she shot a stealthy glance in Nick's direction from beneath her red-gold lashes, another story angle teased and tickled through him, and he realized the reason for this inconvenient fascination.

She was a muse.

His muse, anyway. For the next several days.

SYDNEY LEANED against her hotel room chair after dinner and wrapped her fingers around the phone cord with a smile.

"Miss me?" asked Henry.

"Yes." It was so reassuring to hear Henry's steady voice, and to tell him what he wanted to hear, and to really mean it. If only life could always be this uncomplicated. "Yes, I do. In fact, I was thinking exactly how much I miss you, right before dinner."

"How's the food over there? As bad as they say?"

Her smile dissolved. "It's not that bad."

Henry didn't appreciate foreign cuisines—not that this evening's roast beef, potatoes and peas qualified as exotic. Still, he always managed to don a patient smile and gamely taste all her spicy, impulsive culinary experiments. The fact that he was such a good sport about it made it easier, somehow, for her to sacrifice the exciting foods she loved and prepare the basics he preferred.

She glanced at her watch and stood. "I'd better go. I haven't finished dressing yet, and Gracie's waiting for me in the lounge."

"All right." He paused. "I love you, you know."

"I know." She just hadn't figured out what to do about it yet. Marriage was such a monumentally frightening commitment that even her normal impulsive responses—weaklings that they were—had flown the coop.

But this wasn't the moment to reflect on the situation. And far too many moments had passed as she'd sucked in a breath and prepared to make the expected and logical response. "I love you, too."

"Sydney?"

She winced. Her hesitation hadn't gone unnoticed. "Got to run, Henry. Bye."

She slipped the receiver back into its spot and reached over her shoulder to nab the elusive zipper pull in the back of her dress. No luck. The navy knit sheath was a favorite, but the fastener had been designed for a yoga fanatic. She twisted toward the mirror to improve her aim and relaxed her shoulder joint to gain a fraction of an inch. This time, she caught the zipper—and immediately snagged it in her hair.

"*No.* This is *not* happening." She angled her head to check the damage in the mirror and winced at the tug on her nape. The dress gapped above her shoulder blades, and a hunk of her hair kinked up in a roller-coaster loop.

One of her students quietly rapped at the door—maybe one of the girls, who could fix the problem. Sydney scrunched her neck, tugged at the front of her dress and pulled the doorknob. "Boy, am I glad—"

Nick Martelli lounged in her hotel room doorway.

His gaze swept from her blushing face to her bare toes. "The feeling's mutual," he said.

"I wasn't expecting… I mean, you're not…" Cool air danced over a bit of bra strap exposed in the tangled mess in back, and goose bumps—and other bumps—popped out in inconvenient places.

Why did this man always have to catch her at a disadvantage? So far he'd seen her deranged, clumsy, obsessive and uptight—and now this. And to make matters worse, he seemed to find it all very amusing.

"That's okay, teach," he said with one of his wry grins. "No explanations necessary. That's my assignment. I came to deliver another apology, and a peace offering."

"Another apology?" She hadn't collected the first one. Somehow he'd managed to wiggle his way over and under anything incriminating, in spite of all the traps she'd set for him during dinner. "Now what did you do?"

"Nothing naughty since dessert, I swear."

She clung to the door, wondering how to get rid of him. She had no intention of engaging in a conversation with Nick Martelli, not when she looked like a cross-dressing Quasimodo. And not in her hotel room, not after she'd forbidden her students to entertain members of the opposite sex in theirs.

He held up two soft drink cans. "May I come in?"

"Gracie isn't here, and—"

"Good. I only brought two." He brushed past her in one lithe move and crossed the room to set the cans on a table. She couldn't help admiring his long-legged saunter or the way his shoulders filled out his leather bomber jacket. And she couldn't ignore the disconcerting tightness in her stomach, or the heat that seeped through her. *That's all I need,* she thought. *A physical attraction to the playboy of Student Tours International. The man is pure trouble.*

She opened the door as far as she could and then pressed her back against it, her arms crossed like a shield as he approached.

"Glasses?" he asked.

"Thank you for the gesture, and for the soda, but I really don't have time for this right now. I need to finish getting ready, so if you'll excuse me, I—"

"Looks like I got here just in time." He gently tugged her away from the door, and then he nimbly, neatly untangled her hair and closed her zipper. "That mess looked a little hard to reach," he said as he turned her to face him.

She gazed into eyes as dark as night and framed by smile-crimped lines at the corners, one of them daubed a sickly green beneath a thick, straight brow. He was standing too close, and his hands were too warm on her arms, and his leather and soap scent was too tantalizing for her peace of mind.

The door slipped shut behind them.

"You look completely ready to me," he murmured. "In fact, I can't imagine what you could possibly improve on."

He ran long, lean fingers through her curls, casually combing one forward over her shoulder. Her pulse hammered, too hard, too fast. She needed to get things back under control.

Control. She took a deep breath—and realized how quickly she'd fallen under the spell of his practiced moves and smooth lines. "Thanks for the help," she said, narrowing her eyes. "You certainly seem to know your way around women's zippers."

His hands dropped to his sides. "Sisters."

"Pardon me?"

"Sisters. Just Joe and me holding out against hordes of 'em."

He wandered about her room, snagging a crumpled towel from the floor and folding it neatly over the back of a chair. "I got lots of practice. Buttons, laces, skate keys—I'm a pro." He sorted through the clutter on the dresser, picked up her cologne and sniffed.

"Oh," she said. His casual tour of her personal items was playing havoc with her nervous system, just as his dinner interrogation—and the keen focus of those dark eyes—had played havoc with her appetite. All those questions had seemed intensely personal, not mildly conversational.

She cleared her throat. "Didn't I hear you mention an apology?"

"Yes, you did." He set the bottle down, and his cocky grin snapped back into place. "I should have checked with you first before skipping the museum. I'm sorry for that, and for getting back so late."

"Thank you for..." She frowned. "For understanding."

"Does that mean I'm forgiven?" He slipped his hands into his pockets and scuffed a shoe against the carpet, with no attempt to disguise the fact that he knew he was overplaying the boyish chagrin bit.

She sighed. "Yes, you're forgiven."

"Good." He stepped closer. "Then you'll consider having dinner with me again tomorrow night?"

She stepped back. "We're on a tour. We'll have dinner together every night."

"What I had in mind was something a little more intimate. Just the two of us." He closed the gap between them and toyed with her hair again. "Joe said he'd baby-sit your kids for you."

"Shouldn't you have checked with me first?" She batted his hand aside, setting her temper loose to bubble to the surface. Right now, anger seemed a good way to keep him at a safe distance.

He threw up his hands. "What do I have to do to stay out of trouble with you?"

"What makes you think I want you to do anything at all?"

"Look, Sydney," he said as he paced the room, "we're going to be living in each other's pockets for another week and a half. Sharing the same dining rooms and hotels, the same buses, boats and tours. It would certainly make things more relaxed—more enjoyable—to know that I was on good terms with all the adults in this group."

"*All* the adults? Are you planning a series of intimate dinners for two?" She marched to the dresser and grabbed a comb to tug through her hair. "Oh, except for Joe, of course. He'll be doing all the baby-sitting."

She watched in the mirror as Nick rubbed the back of his neck, staring at the floor. Slowly his eyes lifted. She could observe their progress, feel their touch, as they traveled over the curves outlined by the drape of her dress.

His gaze met hers in the glass. "You know," he murmured, "it's awfully hard to argue with a woman who looks the way you do right now."

Her stomach did a quick jackknife on its way to her knees. She dropped the comb, wincing as it clattered across the dresser's surface. In her hurry to grab it, she knocked over the little bottle of scent and scattered her faux sapphire earrings.

Smooth move, Gordon.

In the mirror, she watched that familiar, wry amusement flicker in Nick's eyes before they darkened and smoldered. Dang, he could do a great smolder. Things were definitely heating up in here. She held her breath, afraid of fanning a stray flame.

He shifted his stance. "Time to start from scratch."

"Okay." She turned and exhaled, smoothing her hands over her dress. Saved from spontaneous combustion—for the time being. "Good idea."

He stalked to the door. "As I recall, I entered, peace offering in hand—the finest light beverage I could find in the neighborhood." He strolled to the table, improvising the little scene. "I even helped you with your zipper—more of that chivalry stuff."

He paused for her reaction. When she rolled her eyes, he shot her a lopsided grin.

"I made a heartfelt apology, which you accepted," he reminded her. "Encouraged by my apparent success at smoothing things between us, I asked you out to dinner."

He slumped, the image of dejection, onto the foot of Gracie's bed. "I can't tell if I'm making any progress here, but at least you're listening." He glanced up. "You are listening, aren't you?"

"Yes." She stifled a smile. "Go on."

"I must really be slipping." He shook his head. "Usually when I ask a woman out to dinner and add a little flattery, she at least considers, instead of looking for ulterior motives." He shot her a dangerous look. "The ulterior motives part is supposed to come after dinner."

"Nick, I already—"

"Let me finish." He held up a hand. "I've tried flattery. I've tried the Boy Scout good deed approach. I've used up about a month's worth of charm. I'm running out of ideas here, Sydney." He focused on the floor. "Maybe a play for pity will work. I'll throw myself at Gracie's feet and beg her to intercede on my behalf."

"You'd probably have a better chance with her, anyway. For some God-knows-why reason, she likes you."

Nick's head snapped up, his smile dazzling. "You two have been talking about me, huh?"

Sydney laughed, charmed in spite of her resolve against it, and pointed to the door. "Out."

He rose and shoved his hands into his pockets. "You're not still mad at me?"

"No."

"Friends?"

"Let's stick with friendly acquaintances for now," she said, opening the door for him.

He strolled through it and turned to face her. "Dinner?"

"Not that friendly." She shut him out, leaned back against the door and stared at the two sodas sitting side by side on the table across the room. There was no mistaking the mush-like quality in the sag of her spine.

CHAPTER FIVE

HARLEY MAXWELL arrived home from her day job dealing blackjack along Lake Tahoe's north shore to find trouble in her usual parking spot and more of it across the street, sprawled on Norma and Syd's front porch. Much more of it. Six feet, three inches of it, to be exact. Trouble in a three-piece navy-blue suit, striped navy-blue tie and serious navy-blue eyes.

She yanked the steering wheel of her tin-can car hard left and tickled the clutch through the familiar cough-and-shudder routine. Her car tried to roll over and play dead, but she stomped on the brakes before it could shimmy off the steep edge of the road. Big mistake. The little engine that usually could up and died.

She climbed out and slammed the compact's door, hard, so it would stick. Had to stay on top of things, show that car who was boss. It might not last long enough to get her to Vegas, once she'd saved enough to make her move, but she was counting on it to get her to her second job that night. Tomorrow she'd have a heart-to-heart with the carburetor. Maybe threaten it with a tune-up from Dusty, the oversize mechanic with the sledgehammer hands and the scary-looking tools. It wasn't much of a threat, really. Dusty was a pushover for down-on-their-luck autos and Harley's apple tarts.

She took a deep breath and prepared to deal with the man lounging near the stairway leading to Syd's attic apartment: Henry Barlow, the oversize attorney with the manicured nails and the nifty leather brief-case. It wasn't going to be easy; Henry wasn't a pushover for anything she could think of. It would take a hell of a lot more than an apple tart to ease her way around him.

She stilled a moment and waited for her heart to do that odd flippy thing it did whenever she saw him. She had no idea why the sight of the terminally re-pressed businessman with an undertaker's fashion sense and a constipated outlook on life could make her heart stutter. Maybe her heart needed a tune-up, too.

Henry sure looked like he could use one. Someone had mussed his hair and loosened his tie. Not too much, or she might not have recognized him, though the sedate silver sedan parked in front of her house was a pretty big clue. The mussing couldn't be Henry's doing. He never mussed—er, messed up. Especially not his appearance. Razor-sharp, that was his personal style. Every tie knotted, every crease pressed, every hair perfectly—and predictably—in place.

She ambled across the narrow, rutted mountain road. "Hey, Hank, what's up?"

"How many times do I have to tell you my name's not Hank?" He struggled upright. "It's Henry."

"Oh, I don't know." She dropped her canvas tote on the step below his feet. "Several hundred more, at least. It's not that I forget your name, you know. It's just that 'Henry' doesn't go down as smooth as 'Hank.'"

"That's ridiculous." He belched, and a whiff of whiskey-soaked misery floated her way. "Henry is meluf…meliful…it's poetic. Hank is a truck driver in North Dakota."

Hank Barlow drunk? In the middle of the afternoon? What was the world coming to? "What are you doing here?" she asked.

"Checking to see if Norma needs any…" He waved a long-fingered hand in the air. "Anything. While Sydney's gone."

Anyone who knew Norma, Syd's retired landlady who lived in the ground level of the Victorian-era house, knew she could take care of herself. Hank's reason for being here was as flimsy as his hold on his dignity.

He dribbled an expensive single malt into the faceted crystal glass in his hand and took a loud, slurping sip.

"For cryin' out loud." Harley shook her head. "Ditch the Waterford and put the booze in the bag. You're embarrassing me here."

He stared at the glass. "I rang Norma's doorbell to ask about Sydney's plants, but she didn't answer."

"Today's Wednesday. Norma's bridge group

meets on Wednesdays." She settled beside him on the sun-warmed porch. "Why don't you come over to my place? I can fix you some coffee while you wait for her. We can have a nice talk. About what's bothering you, for instance."

A jay swooped past with an annoyed squawk to fill the empty spot where Hank's response belonged.

"Syd playing hard to get again?" asked Harley.

"It's only a temporary setback. I'll talk to her and straighten this out when she gets back." He stared into his glass. "I have to marry her. It's an investment in the future."

Harley frowned. "That's one way of putting it, I guess."

"There are a number of important factors to consider. And I've considered them all, very carefully. It's the logical thing to do."

Harley noticed he hadn't mentioned love. But she'd try to be supportive. He was a nice guy, even if he was a little stiff. "Being logical is important in a relationship, I suppose."

"It's good to have someone understand. You're a nice woman, Harley." He tossed back the last drops of whiskey in his glass and set it on the step. "Except when you call me Hank."

"And you're a nice man, Hank." She patted him on the knee. There were some nice, lean muscles under those sharply pleated slacks. Who'd have guessed?

There was a nice, steady heart beating beneath that neatly pressed jacket, too. Hank Barlow was one of the nicest men she'd ever met. That wasn't saying

"Harley?"

"Hmm?"

"This is probably the whiskey, too," he said, and then his mouth pressed against hers.

She froze for a moment, while his lips skimmed a teasing line along hers and his hands drifted down to settle at her waist. She tried—she really tried—to remember that Hank was feeling a little unsteady, that technically he was still Syd's boyfriend and that they were standing in the middle of the street where the neighbors could watch the show. But then his tongue swept inside her mouth, and he pulled her tight against him, and a moan rumbled up from his chest, and she was lost in the delicious, delightful surprise of his kiss.

The surprise had nothing to do with the fact that she'd never imagined this kiss could happen. A girl was entitled to her fantasies, after all. No, the surprise was that there was nothing repressed, or sedate, or stiff, or predictable, or *nice* about this kiss. This kiss was the opposite of nice. It was a take-no-prisoners assault, a seductive and sensual plummet into something dark and deep.

Her heart flipped and flopped one last time, and then it fell into Hank's oversize hands with a thud.

NICK'S FINGERS danced over his laptop's keyboard the morning after the play as he roughed out a scene for his mystery novel. The clack of the keys was faint competition for the whoosh and whir of the traffic noise rising like vapor from the rain-moistened pavement below. He closed his eyes for a moment and inhaled the aroma of early-morning London wafting through his open hotel window. Cooking oil and diesel fuel blended in a cheap scent: Big City.

He clicked the save command and slumped in the chair to read through his draft. Jack Brogan, the star of most of his stories, was moving up in the world, and London would make a classy background for his latest exploits. This could be the start of an entire European series, a project that would require plenty of research. Writing books set in exotic locales could be an exhausting business, but if someone had to do it, it might as well be Nick Martelli.

His thoughts drifted again to the uptight teacher from California. A major mystery there, and his own sleuthing hadn't yet revealed what it was about her— other than her looks and her attitude—that was striking sparks.

Story sparks, among other kinds. He was starting to believe his own theory about her being some kind of muse. And thinking about her the way he usually did—with his cranial blood supply taking a trip south—wasn't the proper way to think about a muse.

Not that he was aware of proper behavior when it came to muses. But he'd bet seducing them wasn't on the program.

Behind him, Joe groaned again, struggling toward complete consciousness. Nick stalked across the room and yanked the pillow out from under his brother's head. "Rise and shine, Mr. Martelli. Breakfast in thirty minutes."

Joe rolled with a yawn and swiped a hand over his morning stubble. "Maybe I'll grow a beard this week."

Joe's wife would kill him if he came home scraggly, and she'd probably have Nick tortured as an accomplice. Connie Martelli was one scary lady.

He chucked the pillow at Joe's head. "Over our dead bodies, and I mean that literally. Shave. Shower. Dress."

Joe closed his eyes and groaned. "God, what a nag."

"Just making sure you don't get homesick," Nick drawled. "And pick up your stuff before we leave. You'll lose something if you don't keep things picked up."

"Yes, hon."

Joe staggered into the bathroom, and a moment later Nick heard one of the sounds of his youth: his brother whistling tunelessly over the tap water.

He reached across the table to snag the tour itinerary. Today's highlights: Stonehenge and Salisbury, followed by another free afternoon. Nick wondered what Joe had planned for his students after lunch. Most likely a pit stop to keep them going until tea time, with a few educational tidbits tucked haphazardly between the snacks.

Joe walked back into the room, rubbing a towel over his thinning hair. "How's the research going? Is

Jack Brogan going to tie up the loose ends in London, or is he going to chase the bad guys all over Europe?"

"Haven't decided that yet."

Joe upended his suitcase over his bed, dumping his clothes in a heap. "I'll bet the girl this time has long orangey hair, big green eyes and legs like a ballerina's."

"Her eyes are blue." Nick closed the laptop. "And what are you getting at?"

"Nothing. I'm just afraid I'm going to trip over your tongue every time Syd walks by."

"Take it back."

Joe pulled a wrinkled shirt over his head. "Or what?"

"Or I won't stick your wallet back in your knapsack the next time it falls out."

"Speaking of which…" Joe pawed through the clothing heap. "Have you seen my khaki shorts?"

Nick twisted in the chair, tugged Joe's shorts from under a Tower of London souvenir bag and tossed them in his direction. "Are your students ready for Mr. Hairy Legs?"

"I'm not even a blip on the radar." Joe stumbled into his shorts. "There are other students here, Nick. Fascinating others, of both sexes. From high schools in exotic places like Albuquerque and Tahoe. I'm surprised you're still sitting next to me on the bus, what with all those pheromones in the air. Especially the California ones."

"You're not going to let this go, are you?" Nick sighed. "I get it. Connie's on your back again. 'Poor

Nicky, all alone with his broken heart. Find him a woman or sleep on the sofa.'"

"It's nothing like that."

Nick stared at him.

"Okay, maybe a little." Joe knelt and reached under his bed for his shoes. "You like her, don't you?"

"Connie? I'm nuts about her. I'll be sorry until the day I die that you saw her first."

Joe rolled his eyes. "Syd. Sydney Gordon. One of the best-looking single women I've seen in a long time. And not just your basic beautiful, but fresh, in that gotta-take-a-second-look kind of way." He waved a shoe for emphasis. "Am I right?"

"So dogs don't howl when she walks by," Nick said. "So what?"

"She's intelligent and creative, too."

"Is there a point to this?" Nick glanced at his watch. "And are we going to get to it before they stop serving breakfast?"

"The point is, you're thirty-six, and you haven't been in a serious relationship for years." Joe sat to pull on his shoes. "It's time to think about your future, Nick. Being everyone's favorite uncle is a dead-end job. You won't be happy if you end up alone. It's time to find someone you can take home to meet Mom."

"And you think Sydney would meet Mom's approval?"

"Definitely." Joe smiled over his shoulder. "Which spells trouble for you."

"No trouble. 'Cause I'm not looking."

"Don't lie to me, Nick. I'll have to hurt you."

"So I peeked a couple of times." He shrugged. "Big deal."

"I'm just looking out for you, little brother." Joe finished dressing and stood. "And looking for a little entertainment while I'm at it. Thing is, even if you put your biggest moves on Syd, she wouldn't give you the time of day."

Nick snorted. "She already knows the time of day in every zone corresponding to the major world capitals. But I suppose this is your subtle way of saying I've lost my touch?"

"Which brings me to point number two," said Joe. "You've lost your touch. You've forgotten how to court a woman. I'm not talking about tossing out some line—I'm talking about making an effort to—" He grunted as he pulled on the second shoe. "You know, do the whole romance thing."

"There's not a woman alive who could give me any kind of trouble for any length of time." Nick winced. "Except Connie. She could make my life hell for all eternity."

"I thought you were nuts about her."

"That's the official line. Off the record, she drives me crazy."

"Connie might drive you crazy," said Joe, "but a woman like Syd could bring you to your knees."

Nick grabbed his backpack and slung it over his shoulder.

"Begging for mercy." Joe stood and clasped his

hands to his chest. "'Marry me, please, and put me out of my misery.'"

"It'll never happen."

"Okay, then." Joe sucked in his gut and put on his serious face. "I dare you. I dare you to romance Sydney Gordon."

"A dare?" Nick rolled his eyes. "Last time I looked, I had a driver's license, selective service registration—you know, all that grown up stuff. I don't do dares anymore."

"I double dare you."

Nick wasn't sure he wanted to mess with the muse mojo. "I hear she has a boyfriend. Which would make taking that dare double dumb."

"I heard it's iffy," said Joe.

"But long-term."

"Which means the guy's a little slow on the uptake."

Nick shook his head. "I'm not making a move on someone else's woman."

"Admirable," said Joe, "but stupid."

"Why her?"

Joe didn't answer. He just gave Nick The Look. The older brother look. The wiser, more wordly, I-want-what's-best-for-you look.

"I've already asked for a date," said Nick. "Twice. Been turned down. Twice."

Joe sighed. "Like I said, you've lost your touch."

Nick wasn't sure he wanted to risk the muse for the woman. But there was a chance—a small, risk-filled, tempting challenge of a chance—that he could have his muse and the woman, too. For the next few days, anyway. Which meant that the boyfriend wasn't an issue. Anything that happened here in Europe would be short-term and G-rated. Fling lite.

And he wouldn't have to put up with any more of Joe's nagging looks.

He cocked his head to one side. "Romance, huh?"

Joe nodded. "Candy and flowers."

"Don't you think that's a little obvious? A little overdone?"

"And you've been having so much success with…?"

"I've been busy," said Nick. "And don't give me that look."

"Hmm." Joe rubbed his chin with a thoughtful look, which wasn't much of an improvement. "There should probably be a kiss. A good one. Women go for that kind of stuff."

"Tongue?"

"Didn't I say a good one?"

Joe opened the door, and they headed into the hall. "One last thing," he said as he hit the button for the elevator. "I like her, Nick. Hurt her, and I'll sic Connie on you."

"You can't bring Connie in on a dare," said Nick. "That's not playing fair. Besides, if I'm going to do this, I'm going to do it for the right reasons."

"And those would be…?"

Nick shifted his pack with a shrug. "I'm working on it."

CHAPTER SIX

SYDNEY SEARCHED for a spot to rest and savor the silence of Stonehenge. Beyond the massive stones, sheep grazed in the silvery sage of the wind-rippled grass. Across the road, smoke drifted from the concession stands. Some of her students, rapidly bored with history's mysteries, queued up for pastries and soft drinks.

She kicked off her sandals and settled cross-legged near the heel stone, smoothing her dress over her knees. The sun's warmth was a welcome caress, and she shifted to let it warm her face. Ah, relaxation at last. She'd been so tense for so many days in a row she thought she might never unwind.

A shadow moved over her—Joe, trying to make an adjustment to his camera strap with one hand while balancing a muffin with the other.

"Here," she said, reaching for the camera. "Let me see that." She quickly coaxed the twisted loop through a tiny plastic catch and handed it back. A lopsided Martelli grin was her reward.

"A woman of many talents," he said.

"One, anyway."

"More than one, I'm sure." He dropped to sit beside her, the camera swinging wildly and his long legs sprawling. The safety of the muffin, however, was never in doubt. "I've never met an actress before."

"Hmm." She swept breeze-tossed curls from her forehead and searched for a way to change the topic. "What about you? Any hidden talents?"

"Nope. What you see is what you get. But Nick's got loads of it." His mouth twisted in an uneven frown. "He just needs to figure out how to put it to good use."

"What do you mean?"

"Never mind. Family sore spot."

"I have to admit," said Sydney, "he strikes me as the black sheep type."

"Martellis don't mess around with that wussy black sheep stuff. We either kill 'em or disown 'em."

"Sounds pretty harsh."

"Natural selection at work. *National Geographic* did a Christmas special the year Massimo stabbed Vito with the turkey baster."

She smiled. "Telling stories must be another Martelli tradition."

"Nick was the one with the wildest imagination. Got him out of a lot of scrapes. Got me into a few."

"I'll bet."

"Just look at him over there." Joe jerked his head toward the buses parked near the concessions stands. Nick moved among a group of Japanese tourists, his crooked smile flashing.

He'd rolled back the sleeves of his shirt, and his dark, sinewy forearms were a striking contrast against the white fabric. A puff of wind ruffled his hair, rearranging the thick layers and tossing a few locks onto his forehead. Even from a distance, she could appreciate his craggy good looks.

She could, but she wouldn't. She'd concentrate on appreciating Henry. Henry was much more handsome than Nick. His features were more classic, his expressions more open and easygoing. There was nothing dark or intense about him.

Not that Henry was bland or boring.

She turned to Joe. "What's he doing?"

"Research. It's a kind of a hobby with him. Everywhere he goes, he talks to people. Collects them, sort of. Asks what they do for a living, how they do it." Joe stretched out on the grass, his hands a pillow for the back of his head, and closed his eyes. "Anything he collects could end up in one of his stories."

"Is he published?"

"Just a couple of short things, but he's working on something longer."

"And he puts things about the people he meets in his stories?"

"Yeah, sometimes." Joe nodded toward the spot where Nick chatted up the tourists. "How they look. How they talk, what they say. Places he's been to, things he's done or heard about. I recognize bits and pieces of things in his stuff, sometimes. It's weird."

So Nick had some *ulterior motives* after all.

Research. Using her as an unwitting subject. "I don't like the idea of serving as a human guinea pig for some character in a book," she said.

Joe glanced sharply at her. "I didn't say that."

"Yes, you did."

"I mean, I sort of did, but I didn't, not really. I didn't say anything about you specifically." He straightened up and turned toward her. "If anyone asks, it didn't come from me."

"Anyone?"

He hesitated. "Nick, for instance."

"You seem awfully worried about this," she said. She stood and gathered her things. "Maybe I should be, too."

"Sydney, wait." He climbed awkwardly to his feet. "You've got this all wrong. There's nothing for you to worry about."

"Because Nick isn't using me as a character in a book?"

"I didn't say he was."

"No, you didn't. But you didn't say he wasn't."

"Damn." Joe tossed his camera strap over his shoulder. "You're not mad, are you?"

"Why would I be mad at you?"

"Not at me." Joe glanced across the road, where Nick was posing for a picture with some of his Japanese lab rats. "At him."

"Why do you care?"

Joe looked miserable. "Crossfire."

"Crossfire?"

"I don't want to get caught in it. I've got a wife and three kids."

"Don't worry," she said, glaring at Nick. "Just duck."

NICK GOT A KICK out of watching Sydney do Europe. He enjoyed the way she noted it down, photographed it and filed it away in her messy tote—after checking her guidebooks to make sure everything was as it should be. She slowly counted her change at the tube stations, and agonized over postcard displays, and bravely sampled the local fare and conscientiously read every plaque they passed. Incredibly, adorably annoying.

She was doing her annoying duty that moment, standing in the nave of Salisbury cathedral and whispering to her students as she pointed to the stained-glass windows.

Beside him, Gracie shook her head. "She's playing tour guide again, isn't she?"

"Looks that way." Nick got a kick out of that, too, although he was glad he wasn't sixteen. If he were, he might develop a crush on his teacher that would cripple him for life.

"She doesn't realize school's out for the summer," said Gracie. "I swear, she studies those guidebooks like there's going to be a test on the plane home."

"Maybe she just wants the kids to get the most out of all this."

"The most what?"

He shrugged. "You've got me there."

Gracie slipped a pair of sunglasses into a deep pink bag. "She's got good instincts. She should just go with those and leave the thinking behind."

"Come on," he said. "Let's catch the rest of the lecture."

As they wandered up the aisle, Sydney pointed toward the center of the nave. "The cathedral spire above us is the tallest in England," she said. "If you lean against one of those big piers that support it, over there, you can look up and see how its weight has actually caused the stone to bend under the strain."

Her students recognized an exit cue when they heard one. "There's an original copy of the Magna Carta on display in the cloisters," she whispered as they fled. "Be sure and take a look."

"Gladys Benson," said Gracie.

"Gladys?" asked Sydney.

"All that stuff about stress and strain and top-heavy weight reminds me of the school secretary."

Nick's laugh was cut short by Sydney's poke in his ribs. "Shh!" she scolded as she tried to shove her guide into a bulging tote. "Remember where you are."

"Sorry." He leaned to whisper in her ear. "You could take me in hand, make sure I behave."

The book tipped and crashed on the floor, followed by a cascade of scattering papers and pamphlets. She fell to her knees and scooped up the mess. When he stooped to help, their heads collided.

"It's Laurel and Hardy," muttered Gracie as her thick, ugly sandals shuffled from view.

Nick picked up one corner of a crumpled map, but Sydney snatched it away, shoving it into her bag.

"We've got to stop meeting like this," he said.

She glared at him and crab-walked to reach for a small plastic case.

He caught her wrist. "Relax."

"I am relaxed," she said, tugging her hand away.

"No, you're not. What's making you so nervous?"

He waited for her to answer, but she turned to the side and swept up a packet of tube tickets. "Is it me?" he asked.

"I don't know what you're talking about."

"Sydney, look at me."

She sat back on her heels and raised her eyes to meet his.

"They're green," he said.

"What?"

"Your eyes. I thought they were blue."

She stood and riffled through the mess at her side, avoiding his gaze. "They're not, actually. They just look like they're different colors sometimes."

"Neat trick." He rose, watching her fuss. "Sydney—"

"I'm in sort of a hurry, Nick. I'd like to see the cloisters, and I want to get a good look at the Magna Carta before it's time to leave and meet the bus. And I want to be sure and pick up some postcards before we leave Salisbury, and then round up the North Sierra kids so they don't keep everyone waiting. There's so much to see and do, don't you think? They sure have us on a tight schedule. Well, better go."

He took her arm before she could step away. "Are you finished babbling?"

"I wasn't babbling." She shook him off and began to neaten a wad of papers.

He watched her flustered attempts to organize her things. "I do make you nervous, don't I?"

"No." She tossed up her chin, and her movements stilled. "You don't."

"Prove it." He stepped closer. "Have a cup of coffee with me. Or some tea, whatever you'd like. This afternoon, when we get back to London. There are some great little cafés in Covent Garden."

"That depends." She shoved the papers back into her tote, giving him a suspicious look. "Are you working on research for one of your stories?"

"What does that have to do with—" A little muscle began to tick along his jaw. *Sabotage.* "Been talking to Joe, by any chance?"

"Joe has nothing to do with this," she said. "I'm perfectly capable of figuring things out on my own. Speaking of which, I was wondering—about the research, I mean." She tilted her head to one side. "There's the kind of research you might do for a setting, like poking around this cathedral. And then there's the kind that gives you ideas for your characters. What they wear, what they say, what they do, right?" She shifted her tote strap over her shoulder. "I wouldn't want to worry about every little thing I say or do."

Nick curled his hands into fists and shoved them into his pockets. He needed to discuss a few things with Joe. Preferably in a dark alley, with no witnesses. "Those little things don't interest me."

She narrowed her eyes. "Guess we can skip the trip to Covent Garden, then. I wouldn't want to bore you."

"*No.* Syd, you—"

"Got to run." She flipped her rose-gold curls over one shoulder. "See you around, Nick." And then she turned and marched toward the center of the nave, her back ramrod straight.

He bit back a curse—considering where he was—and stalked off to find Gracie resting in a choir pew. "Let's go see the damn Magna Carta," he said with a growl.

"Such enthusiasm." She squirmed out of her seat and followed him down the aisle. "I was watching you and Syd. Fangs bared, both of you."

Nick let the oath tumble out. "I've never mangled so many conversations in my life. And the worst of it is, I don't understand how it happens."

He made a donation before they left for the cloisters, and they entered a columned walkway enclosing a simple garden of subdued greenery. Sunshine shafted between stone arches, and the scents of herbs hinted at centuries-old secrets. *Research.* Here he was, surrounded with inspiration and atmosphere for a murder scene, and all he could think about was a woman who got clumsy and defensive every time he got close.

Gracie pulled a packet of gum from her purse. "I can't believe a man like you hasn't figured out the male-to-female attraction ratio."

"The what?"

"You heard me." She fiddled with the wrapper. "It's a scientific theory. Juicy Fruit?"

"No, thanks."

She stuffed a stick of gum into her mouth before dropping the pack back into her purse. "A good-looking man like you sparks an immediate reaction in most women, right?"

"I like to think so. And thank you."

She nodded. "And wasn't it Einstein who said that for every reaction there's an equal and opposite action?"

"Newton," he said. "Something like that."

"Well. There you have it."

"Have what?"

"Pay attention, Nick."

He stopped and stared at her. "You mean, the more a woman is attracted to a man, the harder she tries to fight it?"

"Give the boy an A." Gracie took a seat on a stone bench. "Some women are wary of the immediate physical reaction to a man. They're worried about keeping a lid on all those primitive urges and animal magnetism." She kicked off her sandals and rubbed her feet together. "I'm telling you, this is very scientific—chemical reactions and magnetism and all that stuff."

Nick raised an eyebrow. "What is it you teach?"

"English literature." She wiggled her toes before slipping them back into her sandals. "Where was I? Oh, yes, animal magnetism. Scary stuff, especially for the uptight types. You know—the proper, lady-like types."

"But men and nice women still get together. I know it happens. The world is populated with the evidence."

"There's a very simple—and scientific—solution." She leaned forward. "Stop pushing, Nick. Cool it. Back off."

He frowned. "You mean, ignore her?"

"Got it. It's that 'reaction' thing again." She shifted on the bench. "Look, you ignore her, two things happen. One, she's going to wonder why you've lost interest. Most females want to make sure a male is noticing. It's the female ego. You stop paying attention to her—she's going to start paying attention to you."

Gracie's theory seemed reasonable. Nick didn't know whether to be grateful for her advice or check himself in for psychiatric analysis. He settled beside her on the bench. "And two?"

"With a woman like Sydney, the effect doubles. She's got an overactive conscience, and she's going to wonder if she hurt your feelings or did something wrong. Believe me, when she figures out some way to blame herself for everything, she'll be in a big hurry to make it up to you."

"I don't know about this," he said, frowning. "I like to be honest with a woman. Let her know where

I stand. This attraction-reaction-avoidance stuff sounds like the kind of game men are always accusing women of playing."

"What a pile of manure." Gracie snapped her gum. "Men play just as many games with women, and don't you try to deny it."

He narrowed his eyes at her. "Why do you care so much about Sydney's love life?"

Gracie shrugged. "I like her, too."

"And?"

"I've met her boyfriend. He's a nice enough guy, but he's all wrong for her."

"And you think I'm all right?"

Gracie studied him. "I think you're different."

She stood and slung her purse strap over her shoulder. "Look, are we going to go see the Magna Carta or not?"

"Yeah." Nick sighed. "I can't tell you how much I'm looking forward to seeing a world-famous artifact documenting how a prince of a guy got himself into a hell of a mess."

CHAPTER SEVEN

TWO DAYS LATER, Sydney sprawled on her stomach on her hotel bed, trying to think of something clever to say in her daily postcard to her mother. Scrawling a few words about Windsor castle didn't seem enough for the woman who'd given her a beautiful set of luggage as a bon voyage gift.

The phone rang, and Sydney scooted to the edge of the bed to pick up the receiver. "Hello, this is Ms. Gordon speaking."

"I'm glad you're still answering the phone the way I taught you," said her mother, "in professional situations, anyway."

"Hello, Mother." Sydney's grateful mood began to fade. "How are you?"

"In a hurry." Meredith kept herself busy with a part-time job and charity work, which was fine with Sydney. It kept her too busy to interfere too often in her daughter's life. "I was hoping I'd catch you in. What have you planned for the free evening?"

Sydney bit back a sigh. She'd left her mother an itinerary; she should have known Meredith would be keeping track of their activities. "I'll discuss it with Gracie when she gets back."

"Here's another thing you can discuss with Gracie. A post-tour party."

"A party?"

"A post-tour party. I read about it on the Internet." Meredith outlined an idea for a photo-exchange get-together with the students and their parents a week after they'd returned home. "Think what a good impression it would make on the school board," she said, "and of course you'll have to invite the administrative staff. It would be an excellent way to highlight all you've done for the school. And give them one more reason to consider you for that teaching position."

"You're right—it's a great idea." It was a good idea—a fun one—but she knew her mother wouldn't rest until Sydney followed through, and that it wouldn't be all that much fun in the end.

Sometimes she thought her mother wanted her to get that teaching job more than she did. And she wished her mother trusted her to earn it for herself, because she was a good teacher.

Gracie shoved her way into the room, dropped her Princess Di bag on the floor and slumped against the door.

"Gracie just walked in, so I'd better go," Sydney told her mother. She promised she'd think about the party, and then she dropped the receiver back in its stand.

"That's it," said Gracie. "No more interesting detours. No more souvenir shopping. No more aiming sixteen cameras at sixteen students."

"So, what are we going to do after dinner?" Sydney tucked the postcard into her purse. "It's our last night in London."

"Joe's got plans for one of those Jack the Ripper tours. Dinner, too, at a pub." Gracie staggered toward her bed and collapsed. "The kids are thrilled. Nick's idea, I'll bet."

"Of course." Sydney frowned. "Sounds like fun."

"You don't seem all that excited." Gracie plumped a pillow beneath her head. "Because you don't approve of the idea? Or because it's Nick's?"

"The idea's fine. Just tired, I guess." Tired of that particular subject, anyway. *Nick, Nick, Nick.* "If all the students are going and there are enough chaperones, I think I'll skip it."

"My feet are begging me to stay right where I am, but I can't pass this up," said Gracie. "God, I'm exhausted. Stratford and Windsor yesterday, the British Museum and all that shopping with the girls today— I think we're setting some kind of sightseeing record." She closed her eyes and moaned. "And I miss air-conditioning."

Sydney stood and shoved at the casement window, hoping to increase the chance for a stray breeze by a few inches—and there was London, waiting for her to pay attention. Taxi horns tooting, the scent of curry wafting from the Indian café down the block, the man at the corner convenience store lipping his skinny cigarette and scanning the handwritten headlines posted beside a stack of newspapers. She'd miss it all, but so very much, but Paris beckoned.

She leaned on the sill and craned her neck to watch the students and chaperones gathering in the street below. Nick exited the hotel and sauntered over to join the group. *Nick,* she hmphed. *Nick, Nick, Nick.*

He hadn't cast a single interested-male look in her direction since their chat in the cathedral. Which was fine with her. Really, truly fine. At least she hadn't been subjected to any more of those wolfish once-overs. Or that irritatingly smug charm.

Maybe he'd decided she wasn't worth the trouble. Maybe he didn't find her attractive enough, or interesting enough, or…

As if she cared. And she didn't. Not a bit. She had Henry to think about. Henry and his proposal. And whether she should accept it.

Or not.

She was beginning to wonder why she wasn't missing Henry more, why she wasn't pining for his company or anticipating going back to him. Maybe it was a sign that she didn't love him as much as he deserved to be loved. He certainly deserved someone who'd spend more time thinking about him and less time trying not to think about someone else.

Maybe Henry wasn't the problem, specifically. Maybe the problem was more generic. Maybe she didn't want to get married yet. To Henry, or to anyone else. Maybe she had a case of preengagement jitters. The next few days could be the perfect opportunity to figure things out. She just had to figure out how to do the figuring.

One item was a no-brainer: she wasn't going to do

any quality figuring stuck in a stuffy hotel room on her last night in England.

Last night. Last chance.

"Uhh-nnh." Gracie rolled off her bed with another moan and crossed to the bathroom. "Better freshen up and get going." The door closed behind her with a click.

Sydney plucked one of her guidebooks off the table and thumbed through it, but nothing looked like a cure for the itchy, restless sensation tickling between her shoulder blades. For several days she'd been so good, so responsible, so controlled. Now she felt like a bubbling, steaming teakettle about to scream.

In a sudden rush to experience some unexplored territory, to do some unspecified thing, to flit and flirt and flex her feminine wiles, she hurried to the closet and tossed articles of clothing over her shoulders in search of something fun. Something sexy.

Gracie opened the bathroom door. "What are you doing?

"Looking for a change of clothes."

"What's wrong with the ones you've got on?"

"I want something different. Something fun." Sydney considered a pink T-shirt before flinging it aside. "Something for going out on the town."

"Where exactly are you going?"

"I don't know yet."

Gracie stared at the growing pile of discarded clothes on the floor. "I vaguely remember complaining about all the time you spent organizing your stuff.

Now that I've shared a room with you, I see it's all an act. You've got to be one of the messiest people on the face of the earth."

"I'm packing tomorrow morning, anyway." Sydney poked through the items on the carpet. "This will make it easier to sort through."

"If you say so." Gracie didn't look convinced. "What are you looking for?"

"This," said Sydney as she slipped into a white vest with a row of tiny pearl buttons. "And this," she added, pulling on a short black skirt that flared in several filmy layers.

"I didn't know you had anything in your wardrobe that didn't come down to your ankles," said Gracie.

Sydney ignored the dig. "Where are those dangly earrings? The ones with the black crystals?"

"How you can find anything you own is a mystery to me."

Sydney caught up her hair in a loose twist and shoved a tangle of bangles over one wrist. The vest, cut low in the front, draped suggestively, and the flirty skirt teased around the tops of her knees. She stepped into low-heeled sandals and reached for her cologne.

"Your students may not have a curfew, but you look like you need one." Gracie narrowed her eyes. "What's gotten into you?"

"I don't know," said Sydney. She walked to the door and gave her roommate a reassuring smile. "Just restless, I guess."

"Don't be late."

"Don't wait up."

"Don't forget we've got an early start tomorrow. And you still need to pack."

"Don't worry about me." Sydney turned the knob and opened the door. "I'll probably end up window-shopping in Knightsbridge."

She stepped out into the hall. "Or at a pub, getting an up-close-and-personal sample of British night life. Doing my part to improve international relations."

"Oh, hell," said Gracie, as Sydney closed the door.

SYDNEY TOOK a tube train to the Knightsbridge stop near Harrods and climbed the stairs to the exit. Down the street, the hundreds of bulbs illuminating the huge store's exterior mellowed to ivory in the soft summer evening. Cars and cabs swooped by in an English version of a NASCAR rally, and a Babel of languages in a cosmopolitan mix flowed around her on the jammed sidewalk.

One deep voice rose above the rest. "Good evening."

Sydney turned and studied the carefully groomed man leaning against the doorway of a corner pub. He looked to be about her age and wore the black business suit that seemed to be some sort of uniform near the banking district in The City. "Good evening," she answered.

"Ah, an American." He smiled, displaying lots of long teeth in a narrow jaw.

"That's right."

"From which part of the country?"

"California."

"Really?" He straightened. "Do you live near the beach?"

It was the automatic question that followed the word *California*. "No. In the east, in the mountains."

"One doesn't usually picture that." He hooked a thumb toward the pub door. "Care to come in for a pint?"

She'd wondered if he would ask—and what her answer would be if he did. She stepped through the door, quickly, before she remembered all the reasons she should refuse, and then regretted her impulsive decision a moment later. The concept of a designated smoking section hadn't caught on in English pubs, and she choked on the thick haze.

The crowd was mostly young, mostly hip, and all business. She glanced down at her top and skirt and felt decidedly underdressed for an end-of-the-workday drink.

Her escort led her to a snug booth near the back. "I'm Phillip Aynsley."

"Sydney Gordon," she said as she scooted to the middle of the bench seat. "Glad to meet you."

He loosened his tie before sliding in across from her. "What is it you do in California?"

"I'm a—an actress." Not a lie, exactly. In for a penny, in for a pound—*and this was the country for doing it.*

"Really?" Phillip quirked a dark blond brow. "An actress from California who doesn't live near Hollywood. How *extraordinary.*"

She smiled at the way he drew out the word. *Strawn-ree.* She'd practice it later, letting it sink to the back of her throat and slide over her tongue, sounding oh-so-proper and upper class. "I work in the theater, not in films," she explained as he signaled for a waiter.

She wondered which part she should play tonight. Curious tourist? Femme fatale? Maybe something a little more offbeat.

She decided to treat herself to a little harmless fun, flirting with an attractive man she'd never see again. One performance only—and tonight's Sydney Gordon would be much more interesting than the real thing.

A middle-aged waiter produced two dark ales and an openly admiring smile for Sydney. The drink was terrible, warm and far too malty for her taste. Struggling with the ale and the smoke, she decided the pub experience was one particular bit of English atmosphere she didn't care to absorb.

She sipped her drink bravely, crossed one long leg over the other and prepared to launch tonight's role: Sydney Gordon, free spirit and stage gypsy, fleeing the fallout of an affair with a rock band drummer—an abusive beast of a man named Nick Martelli.

Her audience was appropriately enthralled, aghast, sympathetic and, after an hour's visit, ready to move on to the evening's finale. "It's getting a bit late," he said.

"And I have early-morning plans."

"I'm sorry to hear that," said Phillip. "I was about

to propose a late supper at a club I know, and perhaps a spot of dancing."

"Sounds fun, but...I'm so terribly bored with the club scene, you know?" She dropped her napkin on the table and seized on the chance to escape from the suffocating smoke and the dark brown stuff in her glass.

"Then allow me to escort you to your hotel. It would give us a chance to continue our visit."

He reached across the table and skimmed a manicured hand over hers. "You're a fascinating woman, Sydney."

CHAPTER EIGHT

SYDNEY HAD NEVER been called *fascinating*. She mentally collected the verbal trophy for tonight's performance and, flushed with the small victory, agreed to his offer.

"Do you have a wrap?" he asked as they reached the door.

"No. But I'm fine, really," she insisted, even as the night breeze rubbed goose bumps along her bare arms.

Phillip ignored her protest and slipped his suit jacket around her shoulders. The scent of his cologne on the fabric seemed strangely intimate, and she flinched at his light touch at her back. He guided her to a shiny black Jaguar.

"What a beautiful car," she said.

"A bit of an indulgence, I'm afraid." He helped her in and shoved her door closed with an expensive-sounding *whoosh*. She sank into the leather, grateful that Phillip's offer of an escort didn't include public transportation.

"The depreciation on this model doesn't justify the purchase price," he continued as he settled behind the wheel. "I'm usually a bit more conservative with my investments."

Which he proceeded to explain in numbing detail. *Investments.* Another coin-counting stock market fan. First Henry, now Phillip. She seemed to be a magnet for men like that.

Which was probably a good thing, she told herself with a resigned sigh.

The car glided to a stop a few blocks past the glare of Piccadilly Circus, and she rolled her head to the side, staring out the passenger window. A handsome young couple in dark business suits stepped into the narrow band of light beneath a corner street lamp. The man leaned close to the woman, as if to whisper something in her ear, and she tilted her face toward his. He smiled and slipped an arm around her waist, bending her back to capture her mouth in a fierce kiss.

She pressed against him and seized his coat lapels for balance as she wobbled on her heels, and her pale hair swung in a shining arc beneath the street-light. Their suits seemed to meld in a single dark shadow, and their briefcases swayed, colliding unnoticed.

Sydney bit back a sentimental sigh. She'd once felt the way that couple looked, had known that carefree abandon, that complete absorption in another person. The giddy thrills, the dizzying highs—and the crashing, crushing death of a breathless, mindless passion.

And now she had Henry. Though she'd never shared a moment like that with him—and doubted she ever would—she could still appreciate what she'd found: a perfect man who professed to love her very, very much.

She'd call him when she returned to her room and tell him she loved him, too. She owed him an apology for her moodiness during the past few days.

Feeling much more settled, she hopped out of the car when Phillip pulled to a stop near the hotel's entrance, intent on returning his jacket and murmuring a few quick thank yous. But he insisted, with quietly stubborn British courtesy, on escorting her to her door.

Several embarrassing scenarios flickered through Sydney's imagination as he took her arm and guided her up the marble entrance steps, and all of them involved treating her fellow tour members to a scene featuring her post-curfew arrival with the foreigner she had picked up in a bar. Tonight's performance had just gone sour.

Except for the balding clerk behind the reception counter, the lobby was empty. She breathed a silent prayer of thanks and pulled her key from her bag as Phillip slowly slipped his jacket from her shoulders and folded her hand into his elbow. But she held her breath as they approached the elevators, counting the steps to a safe and unobserved escape.

From the darkened lounge came the subtle clink of ice against glass. Sydney glanced over her shoulder to see a pair of jeans-clad legs sprawled across the rug. Familiar legs, long, lean legs she'd seen stretched across the aisle of the tour bus.

Nick Martelli, sunk deep in the wide-winged comfort of a lounge chair, was definitely noticing her tonight. His dark gaze swept over her sandals, traced a path up her legs to focus on the hemline of her skirt and then paused for a leisurely examination of the drape of her vest.

She nearly felt that gaze brushing along her skin, skimming the deep V of her top, outlining the hollows of her throat and the curves of her features, and she blushed beneath its heat. He took a long, slow sip of his drink, staring at her over the rim of his glass, lapping her up with his eyes.

Phillip's slight tug reminded her that her hand was tucked into the crook of his elbow. She told herself she had nothing to blush over and braced for the mocking twist of Nick's grin. But there was a different set to his mouth tonight, something grim and determined. And there was something different about his expression, too—something disapproving and possessive. His eyes narrowed with a cool, black glitter and a tiny muscle ticked in his cheek.

This was a new Nick. A dangerous Nick. The kind of Nick who was a logical match for the faded bruises and healing cuts, for the coarse layer of stubble shadowing his jaw. She shivered with apprehension and— God help her—a tiny slice of anticipation.

What was wrong with her tonight? She wasn't the kind of woman who went for the dangerous kind of man. No worn black leather, no illegally concealed weapons, no fast sports cars, no quick and desperate couplings in seedy alleyways. Nick looked like he'd just come from that world and was headed back soon. So why was she suddenly tempted to go along for the ride?

To her dismay, he set his glass on a table, slowly rose and strolled toward them, stopping beside Phillip at the elevator. His moves were casual, but she could sense the tension that emanated from him. She caught her breath and waited, trapped in his steely gaze, her pulse stuttering.

He leaned a shoulder against the wall and crossed his arms over his chest. "Hi, Syd."

"Hi, Nick," she answered in a faint voice.

"Nick?" asked Phillip, turning to face Sydney. "This is Nick?"

Nick. The crazed rock musician. She stifled a mortified groan.

"Nick Martelli, yeah." Nick didn't take his eyes off her as he answered Phillip's question. "Got a problem with that?"

Phillip shoved her behind him and held up a hand. "See here, Nick. I don't believe Sydney wishes to see you right now."

One corner of Nick's mouth lifted in an ugly semblance of a smile, and he straightened and stepped in close, stopping when Phillip's upraised hand grazed his chest. "Is that so?" he asked in a silky, threatening voice.

"Yes." Phillip cleared his throat, but didn't lower his hand. "I believe so, yes."

The elevator's little bell sounded its cheerful bing and the door opened. No one moved.

Sydney heard something that sounded like the kind of squeak a mouse might make right before it got stepped on. She thought it might have come from her.

Nick leaned forward, pressing against Phillip's hand. "And why would that be?"

"She came here to get away from you."

Nick moved Phillip's hand aside. "From me?"

"Nick, don't." She tried to edge around Phillip, but he shifted, blocking her. This was playing out like a bad scene in a second-rate play, but it was all too real. "Please," she begged.

Nick narrowed his eyes at her. "Please don't what?"

Phillip's hand shot back up, and Nick's fingers curled into fists.

The elevator door began to close. Sydney stabbed at the button and breathed a sigh of relief when the door shuddered open again. "Whatever it is you're thinking of doing," she said.

"And what would that be?" asked Nick.

"I say," called the clerk from the reception desk. "Is there a problem with the elevator?"

"No," said Sydney. "No problem. Right, Nick?"

"No problem at all." He jerked his head toward the elevator. "Get in, Syd."

"Wait." Phillip took her arm, preventing her escape. The door slid shut. She tugged free and punched at the buttons in a panic. Nothing happened for a moment, and then she could hear the rumble of the car moving up, up and away. *Oh dear oh dear oh dear.*

"You don't have to go anywhere with this man," said Phillip. "You can come home with me. I'll keep you safe."

"Safe?" asked Nick. "Safe from what?"

"From you," said Phillip.

Sydney leaned her head against the elevator door, wishing it would open, *now,* so she could disappear down the shaft.

"Would anyone like any assistance?" asked the clerk. He stepped from behind the counter. "I can call for assistance."

"Thank you," said Phillip. "That won't be necessary."

She jerked back as a faint rumble grew louder. A few seconds later the little bell clanged and the door opened. "The elevator's fine. We're getting on, right now."

She jumped inside, grabbed Nick's sleeve and yanked him in, too. "Good night, Phillip, and—"

The door shut, cutting off the rest of her words. "Thank you," she said to her wavery, metallic reflection.

"Safe?" Nick fisted his hands on his hips and leaned toward her to glare from uncomfortably close range. *"From me?"*

She stepped back. "Let me explain—"

"What is this—some new variation on the luggage thief routine?"

"That was a simple misunderstanding," she said, morphing from mortified to mad and shifting to the offensive. "What is it with you? What did you think you were doing back there?"

The elevator slowed to a stop, and the door opened. "Is that how you got beat up? Is that what happened to your eye?" she asked. "Did you pick a fight with somebody?"

An elderly couple stood in the hotel hallway, staring anxiously at Nick. No one moved. The doors slid closed, and the car continued its ascent.

"No, that's not what happened." Nick pointed at the door. "And you obviously weren't paying attention down there, because I wasn't the one starting the fight."

She angled her chin toward his. "Oh, no?"

He leaned in, nose-to-nose. *"No."*

"I see." Her eyes narrowed to slits. "You just decided you were going to finish it, is that what you were thinking?"

"No, that's not what I was thinking."

"Oh, yeah?"

"Yeah," he said. "You want to know what it is I'm thinking right now?"

Something was crackling in the air between them, something other than temper and ego. Something dark and thrilling, like whatever it was she'd sensed in the lobby. Something she decided to ignore, because she needed to concentrate on her next words instead of wondering what was making her heart pump and her breath catch and her skin feel like she was trapped in a blast furnace. *"Yeah,"* she said, layering on the sarcasm. "I can hardly wait."

"Good." He wrapped his long fingers around her arms and hauled her against him. "Me, too."

She could have fought him off. She was hot enough, and hyped enough, to shove him away and give him another bruise to add to his collection.

But the problem was she was also hot and hyped enough to want him to put his mouth on her. All over her. Right now. Fast and hard and wet and…

The elevator dinged. The door slid back like a stage curtain, and there she was, wrapped in Nick's arms while Eric, Matt and two of the Philadelphia girls stood in the hotel corridor, their eyes and their mouths wide-open with shock.

"Ms. Gordon," said Matt. "We were just, uh…"

"Skipping out on curfew?" Nick released Sydney and pressed a hand against the elevator opening.

"Uh, no," said Eric. "Not us."

The girls shook their heads.

"Right," said Nick. "I didn't think so."

He looked over his shoulder at Sydney. "I didn't see any students trying to get on this elevator to go out somewhere after curfew. Did you?"

"I don't think—"

He shook his head and turned to face the students. "And you guys didn't see Ms. Gordon or me, either. Did you?"

"No," said the girls.

"We didn't see nothing," said Matt.

"Because we weren't here, right?" said Eric. "We were in our rooms."

"Yeah," said Matt. "Nothing happened."

"Good night," said Nick.

"Right." Eric nodded. "Good night."

"Good night," said the girls.

Nick lowered his hand to let the door close and then turned to face Sydney. "What do you mean, 'I don't think'? I was trying to save your professional hide just now. Not to mention handling the chaperoning chores."

"No one asked you to handle my chaperoning for me. And my hide was doing just fine before you grabbed it."

"Don't worry—your hide is safe." He shoved his hands into his pockets. "I won't make that mistake again."

"Thank God."

The door opened on Sydney's floor, and she stepped out. "Nick, I—"

He punched a button, and the last thing she saw as the door slid shut was his angry, heated stare.

She closed her eyes and tried very hard not to erupt in a fireworks display of sexual frustration in the hotel hallway.

Oh. My. God.

CHAPTER NINE

"Excuse me…Henry?"

Henry glanced up from the assets itemization documents arranged neatly on his desk. Barbara, the firm's receptionist—yet another of the matronly women in his life—stood in his office doorway. "There's a young woman here to see you," she said.

He hauled his thoughts up from the depths of estate planning to consider a possible reason for this interruption. "That's odd," he said. "I don't have any appointments scheduled."

"I know." Barbara's upper lip kinked in a disapproving twitch. "She doesn't have one."

He raised an eyebrow and waited.

"She says it's *personal*."

The tone of Barbara's voice told him she didn't think such a thing was possible.

He dropped his pen and leaned back in his chair, curious about who had the receptionist's lip in such a twist. "Show her in, please."

"All right." Barbara hesitated, fiddling with the glasses tethered on a chain around her neck, giving him one last chance to change his mind. "I asked her to wait in the reception area. I'll bring her back."

Straightening his tie, he stood and walked across his roomy office. He preferred to greet his clients and guests at the door rather than from behind the wide, glossy expanse of his desk. First impressions were important, and he always tried to make a welcoming one.

The door opened. Barbara ushered in his surprise visitor, and his smile froze at half-mast. *"Harley."*

"Hey there, Hank." She flapped a friendly little wave at him as she sauntered into the room. Behind her, Barbara's lip danced the fandango.

Harley moved deeper into his office, heading toward the window, a splash of casino neon in a leather-and-mahogany world. Her too-tight T-shirt and her too-short shorts were as out-of-place as the cheeky slap of her flip-flops. A wrinkled brown paper bag dangling from her hands where they were clasped behind her back, and an abstract silver pendant gleamed against the smooth, shadowy V of her cleavage.

He jerked his gaze from the pendant. He had no business admiring someone's cleav—er, chest. Not when he had Sydney's chest to—not when Sydney wasn't here to—not when—

Harley leaned forward to study the notation beneath his framed Kadinsky print, and her ragged denim shorts rode up the backs of her long, tanned legs.

Damn. As an alternative focal point, her thighs weren't much of an improvement. And wasn't that a shame, because they were very attractive thighs.

Muscle, bone and skin arranged in an absolutely fascinating way.

"Real nice place you've got here," she said, and then she straightened and shot him one of her wide, infectious grins. She seemed to have more teeth than most people and flashed them around a lot. "Real nice."

Barbara stiffened at the door. "Would you like something to drink, Ms. Maxwell?"

"That won't be necessary," said Henry, before Harley could answer. "I'm sure this won't take long."

Barbara cast one last daggered glance at Harley and closed the door behind her. Harley stared at the spot where the receptionist had stood and crossed her eyes.

Henry struggled to hide a smile. "What can I do for you?" he asked.

"Nothing." She edged a hip on the top of his desk and set the paper sack next to her thigh. Her long, sleek, tanned thigh.

Henry had never noticed how shapely Harley's legs were before. Sure, he'd looked once or twice, because they were worth a look. Today he thought they looked like a showgirl's. Not that he was an expert on showgirls' legs. But he imagined they must look like Harley's. Very, very nice.

But not as nice as Sydney's, he told himself, and dragged his gaze up to Harley's face.

"I thought you'd want this back," she said, "but I didn't know how to get a hold of you." She patted the brown bag. He waited for her to finish.

"You left it," she said. "You know…the other day." Her eyes darted back to the artwork on the wall, and she pressed her lips together in a thin line.

He realized she was embarrassed, and a little spurt of guilt trickled through him. He hadn't once considered how Sydney's friend and neighbor might feel about the kissing incident. Disloyal and dismayed, most likely. "I'm sorry," he said.

"It's okay." She lifted a shoulder in a shrug. "Turns out this place is close to the post office, and I had to go there anyway, so it's no big deal."

"Thank you." He moved the bag to one side of his desk and felt the weight of his cocktail glass through the paper. "But making you go out of your way to return this to me isn't what I'm apologizing for."

"Oh." She stared at the hands she'd clasped in her lap. "Well. That's okay, too."

He battled back a strange longing to reach out, to slide a knuckle under her chin and lift her face so he could stare into her eyes. They were the same color as his whiskey, he realized. Rich and warm and layered with gold highlights. He flexed and straightened his fingers at his sides, and then he stepped behind his desk so that the width of its surface could stretch like an ocean between them.

A tactical error. His new position gave him a terrific view of the curve of her waist.

He cleared his throat. "I hope I didn't offend you."

"Nope." She glanced over her shoulder at him, through her lashes. Their usual coat of black gunk was missing today. Without the thick, harsh layers of makeup she looked younger. Almost…wholesome.

In a bleached-blond, thrift-shop sort of way.

"No offense taken," she said. "Don't worry about it."

"All right." He tapped a finger against the edge of his desk. "Well, I…I thank you, again, for going out of your way to return this to me, and—"

His office door opened, and Martin Brandwyn, cofounder of the firm, strode in. Slim and silvered and only slightly stooped with age, Brandwyn had mentored and maneuvered Henry into his current position as the most likely candidate for the next full partnership.

Harley slipped off the desk with a little squeak and tugged at the hem of her shorts. Brandwyn watched her jerky move, his watery eyes narrowing slightly. "Pardon me," he said, raising a bushy eyebrow at Henry, "I didn't realize you were in a meeting. With a client."

Henry straightened his tie again. "Harley Maxwell," he said, "allow me to present Martin Brandwyn."

Harley extended her hand with one of her sunny smiles. "Pleased to meet you, Martin."

"The pleasure is all mine, Miss Maxwell." Martin's sharply assessing expression didn't quite match the bland tone of his voice. "It is Miss, isn't it?"

"Yes." She tossed her hair over her shoulder with

a little shake of her head. "But I'm not a client. I'm a friend. Of Hank's."

"Harley is Sydney's neighbor," said Henry.

"Ah, I see." Brandwyn's smile warmed several degrees. "A wonderful young woman, Sydney. And the subject of my visit, in a manner of speaking."

"Well, don't mind me," said Harley. "I was just going."

Henry walked her to the door.

"Nice meeting you, Martin," she said with another smile for Brandwyn, and then she paused in the doorway. "See you around, Hank."

"Yes. Around," Henry said. "And thanks again."

"No problem." She wiggled her fingers at him in a little wave, tossed another grin at Brandwyn and sashayed down the hall toward the reception area.

It looked like a sashay. Henry couldn't be sure, but he thought the way her hips swung back and forth like an upside-down metronome might qualify. He stood and enjoyed the view for a moment longer than he probably should have and then closed the door.

"Hank?" Brandwyn frowned.

"Just a little neighborly joke." Henry slid his hands into his pockets. "What's this about Sydney?"

"Ah, yes." Brandwyn cast a none-too-subtle glance at the door. "Your fiancée is out of town for the next several days."

Henry smothered his frustration over the situation—along with his guilt, confusion and worry. He knew it wasn't right to blame all his problems with

Sydney on this Europe tour, but he sure as hell wanted to. "Technically she's not my fiancée."

"Not at the moment, no. But I assume she soon will be. It's my understanding you have plans."

"I do. And yes, I hope to convince her to become my fiancée. My wife."

Brandwyn's bushy brows crowded together over the bridge of his nose. "Hoping and wishing don't cut it, Barlow."

"No, sir." Henry braced for The Happen Lecture.

"Things happen because we make them happen."

"Yes, sir."

"If you want something to happen, you'll find a way to make it happen."

"I will, sir."

"Glad to hear it." Brandwyn nodded, seemingly satisfied that at least one person in the room had made something happen. "Now, the reason for my visit. Brenda and I have invited the partners and their wives to dinner tomorrow night, and we'd like you to join us."

"Thank you, sir." This was what Henry had been working toward since his first day at the firm. All he had to do was negotiate the final steps in the dance, and the partnership was his. He curled his fingers inside his pockets and squeezed.

"It's unfortunate that your fiancée is out of town," said Brandwyn, frowning. "Brenda enjoyed meeting her at the…what was that event again?"

"The community theater benefit."

"Ah, yes. The theater." Brandwyn's eyes narrowed, and Henry imagined he'd glimpsed a hint of distaste.

"The arts are a valuable asset to a community." Brandwyn paused and lifted an eyebrow. "Although I suppose there are those who might not wish a member of their own family to be involved too intimately in certain creative pursuits."

"I'm sure you're right, sir." Henry cleared his throat. "There's a proper time and place for creativity."

Brandwyn studied him, and his frown deepened. "Sometimes, Barlow, I don't quite know what to make of you."

"Sir?"

Brandwyn waved away the question. "Well, then. Tomorrow night? Seven?"

"I'll be there." Henry opened his door and stepped aside. "Thank you, sir."

"You're welcome." Brandwyn paused on his way out. "Hank?"

"Miss Maxwell has a rather warped sense of humor."

"Yes." The old man's mouth twitched. "But rather nice legs."

"I hadn't noticed, sir."

Brandwyn laughed and slapped him on the shoulder. "Spoken like a man whose nearly-a-fiancée is out of town. Well done, Barlow."

"Thank you, sir."

After Brandwyn had shuffled down the hall and disappeared around the corner, Henry closed his office door and sat at his desk. He stared for several minutes at the wrinkled brown paper sack, and then he scooped it into a drawer and sank back into the depths of the Grundbock estate.

"JUICY FRUIT?"

Nick lowered his *USA TODAY* early on the morning of the scheduled departure for Paris and glared over the paper's edge at Gracie. He'd been sitting in the lobby, reading the same paragraph over and over again while scenes and sensations from the previous evening played in his head. The vision of Phillip's hand on Sydney's arm. The white-hot anger pumping through him when the Brit had shoved her out of range. The soft, ripe feel of her when he'd pulled her into his arms. The confusion in her eyes as he'd lowered his mouth toward hers. His own confusion about what had nearly happened—and how much he wanted it to happen again. *Why* he wanted it to happen again.

He frowned at Gracie's pack of gum. "Isn't it a little early in the day for that?" he asked.

She shrugged and dropped it back in her case. "I suppose I should cut back. I'm working my way up to a pack a day."

"Former smoker?"

"Yep."

"I may not be interested in increasing my chewing enjoyment right now," he said as he folded the paper and set it aside, "but I was hoping you and I could have a talk about some of your scientific theories."

"Love to join you, but I can't." She sighed. "I'm looking for Edward. I have to ask if he can delay our departure for a few hours. I don't think my roommate can be packed anytime before noon."

Nick's irritation drained away. "Is she sick?"

"No, no." Gracie shook her head. "Just having a little trouble getting organized."

"Syd? Having trouble with organization?"

"If you only knew." Gracie sighed again and shot him a sly, sideways glance. "She was out rather late last night."

"I know."

"You saw her come in?"

"Don't play games, Gracie." He narrowed his eyes at her. "You probably pumped her for every detail."

"The well ran dry before we got to the good stuff." She grinned. "Maybe you'd like to fill me in?"

He all but growled.

"Okay," she said. "Maybe this is the time to end the silent treatment. She's already upset, I can tell."

"It's probably all that *guilt* she's feeling," said Nick.

"Why would Syd be feeling guilty?" Gracie's smile was angelic. "She's an attractive single lady who had some time to herself. Sounds like she had a lot of fun. Until she got back here, that is."

"What about her boyfriend back home?"

"What about him?"

Nick shifted forward and paused, cursing his overpowering curiosity and kicking himself for being weak enough to pry. "What's the story there?"

"Why do you want to know?"

He ground his teeth.

Gracie looked around the dining room. "Where's Joe?"

Nick settled back with an angelic smile of his own. "Hiding."

CHAPTER TEN

SYDNEY STROLLED down the Boulevard des Batignolles shortly after the tour group had checked into their Paris hotel, itemizing her first impressions of the city. Early customers lounged over their wine at tiny café tables as sagging matrons trudged past, crusty baguettes poking out of the white grocery bags swinging at their sides. Above colorful awnings, lacy grillwork sprouted from balconies and dormer windows punctuated mansard roofs.

She checked her watch at a corner while she waited for the traffic signal to change, wondering how much longer her errand would take. The grouchy concierge must have enjoyed his private joke, sending her off on a mile-long errand. Surely there'd been an automated teller machine closer to the hotel.

It was her own fault. She'd been so intent on avoiding Nick Martelli that morning—during the departure from London, and the bus ride to Dover, and the short cruise on the ferry, and the transfer to their hotel—that she'd forgotten to change her currency. Now she needed some euros, and she needed them fast.

Nick. Even now, the memory of those moments in the elevator set her pulse racing and heated her cheeks. She hadn't called Henry when she'd returned to her room—she'd had no idea what to say. What to do.

What to *feel.*

Lost in her thoughts, she nearly missed the signal change and crossed in front of an impatient driver. Wincing at the bleat of the horn behind her, she stepped to the curb on the other side and nearly collided with a man outside a red-shuttered tabac shop.

He began to walk beside her, staring at her clothes, her hands, her hair, her purse. Sydney picked up her pace, but the man lengthened his stride, maintaining his position next to her.

She snuck another uneasy glance at him. Dark, receding hair slicked back from his thin, sallow face to disappear under the collar of a tight polyester jacket with garishly contrasting stitching. The faded jeans below the jacket were even tighter.

He began to speak to her—in French, she thought. She tightened her grip on her purse and walked still faster, her legs and back aching with tension, but he moved closer to her side. She wondered if she should stop and explain that she didn't understand. No, it would be better to ignore him and walk even faster. Surely he'd lose interest eventually.

She focused on the signal at the street corner ahead, mentally begging it to stay green. She was uncomfortably aware of the pungent aroma of the stranger's clothes and cigarette, of the oily sheen of his hair, of the hundreds of euros in her wallet, of the fact that no one in her tour group knew exactly where she was at this moment, of her inability to communicate with any of the people around her. Those she passed seemed to stare coldly at her, at her and the man who could now easily reach out and touch her. Sydney wondered if they could hear what he was saying to her, what his words meant.

The signal changed. She nearly stumbled to a stop, her chest tight with anxiety, her knuckles white from her grip on the purse strap. He stepped in front of her, his eyes insolently roaming from her blouse to her purse, to the necklace around her throat, and then he spoke again with a yellow, gap-toothed smile. He leaned in close, and she stepped back, brushing against a café table. The stranger muttered something to the table's occupants, and they chuckled with him. She shifted to the side, but he cut off her escape route, backing her toward the darkened area beneath the green-and-white striped awning.

"Sydney!" Nick jogged into the dining area and swept her up in a smothering hug. He kissed her hard on the cheek and whispered in her ear, "Pretend you love me or we may both be in trouble here."

"*Nick!*" She threw her arms around his neck. Panic and relief overrode any lingering embarrassment over her behavior during last night's argument, and she held on tight. He felt solid and safe and oh, so good. So right. So surprisingly right. Everything in her calmed and stilled for a moment, and then kicked back up in an emotional reaction of a different sort. A confusing sort.

He tightened his hold on her, and she squeezed her eyes shut and burrowed her nose into his shirt collar. She was upset. She'd had a scare. She shouldn't be noticing things like the delicious scent of his skin or the rasp of his whiskers against her cheek, or the width of his shoulders or the way his hair waved around his nape. But she was noticing—boy, oh boy, was she noticing.

"Wow." He pried her arms from around her neck. "That was some pretty good pretending."

Wrapping an arm tightly around her waist, he turned to the café crowd, shrugged a Gallic-size shrug and announced something in French they all found terribly amusing. The short, greasy man turned toward the walk and disappeared.

Nick cupped his free hand under her chin and pulled her face close to his. "You okay, Syd?"

She nodded. "Let's get out of here."

He kept her tucked against his side, and she leaned her head on his shoulder as they made their way down the boulevard. His oversize shape seemed to mold to her like a big, warm blanket, comfortable and secure. Steady. Funny, she'd never thought of him that way before. She took a couple of deep breaths as the adrenaline began to drain away.

When she lifted her head, he edged away and took her hand to tug her around a corner into a quieter side street. And then he paused in front of a patisserie and let her go, shoving his hands into his pockets and focusing on the gooey pastries in the window display.

She was surprised how much she wanted to be tucked against him again.

"That was quite a little scene back, there," she said. "Ever thought of taking up acting?"

"I was pretty awesome, wasn't I? Considering I was scared out of my wits." He scrubbed his hands over his face. "That must explain it. Scared crazy. Crazed. Whatever."

He flung out his arms and paced a tight circle. "God, Sydney. What did you think you were doing?"

"What do you mean, what was I doing?" She took a deep breath and concentrated on lowering her voice. She was trying to be grateful here, and shouting wasn't the best way to get that across. Besides, she'd nearly shouted at him last night, and she didn't want it to become a habit, even though something about him tended to send her responses into overdrive. "I didn't do anything."

"You took off without letting anyone know where you were going, or when you'd be back."

She crossed her arms over her chest. "I can take care of myself."

He snorted. "Yeah, it looked like it back there."

"Stop yelling at me."

"This isn't yelling," he yelled. "When I yell at you, you'll damn well know it."

The hell with gratitude. She narrowed her eyes. "What makes you think you're ever going to get that chance?"

He threw up his hands with a growl and stalked down the street in the general direction of the hotel.

"Nick!" She ran to catch up. They couldn't end another discussion like this. Not now, not after those moments when he'd scooped her up and she'd felt…the way she'd felt. "*Nick.* Wait up."

He stopped, shoved his hands back into his pockets and glared at her.

"Thanks for coming along when you did," she said. "I really appreciate it. And you're right—I shouldn't have gone off alone."

He rolled his eyes. "Thank you, God."

"But how did you find me? I didn't see you in the lobby when I left."

"Edward had some brochures for you, but he couldn't find you. I checked with your kids, and then with the concierge."

"So you went looking for me?" She remembered the oily little man and shivered. "I'm lucky you found me when you did."

"Not so lucky." He shrugged. "Just slow."

"What do you mean, *slow?*"

"I caught up with you a while back. You were busy playing the tourist, looking at this, looking at that, getting in everyone's way. Almost getting flattened in traffic." He frowned. "Driving me nuts."

"You followed me?"

"Only for a few blocks."

"But you followed me," she said. "You were *spying on me.*"

He pulled himself up straight. "I wasn't spying."

"Okay, you were just following me. Like some kind of *stalker*."

"Not a stalker. More like a private investigator."

"Ooh!" She clenched her teeth and fisted her hands as her blood pressure spiked. "It's all just some big game to you, isn't it? Some big—wait, no, I get it now. *Research*. That's what this was all about, right? *Research for your book*."

"No." He shifted his stance. "Not exactly."

She thought for another moment about what he'd been doing, and what had happened, and her temper flared. "You saw that man bothering me, and you didn't come and help me out."

"How could I be sure you weren't just picking up another foreign acquaintance?"

She gave him an abbreviated version of her death stare and started down the street toward the hotel.

"Syd," he called, jogging behind her. "*Syd*. Wait up."

She shook her head and kept moving, "I owe you my gratitude, not my company."

"That's cold."

"That's not cold. When I'm cold, you'll damn well know it."

He grabbed her arm and spun her around. *"Sydney."*

"Let go, Martelli." She twisted away and raised her hand to adjust her purse strap.

He ducked out of range. "Not the purse. Anything but the purse."

"Tempting, but I left all my bricks back at the hotel."

He stepped back in close, and she stood her ground.

"Lady," he said, wagging a finger under her nose, "you're a hell of a lot of trouble."

She tossed up her chin. "So why bother?"

His finger froze in midair. "I have no idea."

He stood so close she could see his mood shift from anger, to amusement, to…something else. Something that started crackling in the air between them again. She could practically see the sparks. His eyes grew dark, the tension in his jaw eased, his mouth softened, and that strange sexual tractor beam of his started humming its way in her direction. She had to escape before it locked on target.

His eyes dropped to her lips. Too late.

If he kissed her now, she wouldn't put up a struggle. She might bite his lip, but not too hard. Just hard enough to let him know she didn't want him to kiss her.

Or did she?

Oh, dear.

Think of Henry.

Sheesh. It was like telling herself to close her eyes and think of England.

Nick edged a bit closer, and she swayed a bit forward, and his hand lowered to her arm. His touch set off fire alarms, and she realized she didn't want to think of Henry, not at the moment. She wanted

Nick's kiss, wanted his touch. In fact, she wanted a whole lot more.

She wanted Nick. And she was pretty sure he wanted her, too.

One corner of his mouth quirked up in one of his crooked grins. "Why do I bother with you?"

"What do you want?" She smiled back. "A hint?"

"No." He let go of her arm and took a step back. "Nothing."

She tumbled off the sensual cloud she'd been drifting on and crashed at Parisian street level. She'd been about to betray Henry—just a little, anyway— and for what? A guy who could shift from come-on to stand-down at a moment's notice. *"Nothing?"*

"Okay, not nothing. Something."

"Something?"

He glanced at her. "A date?"

"Are you asking my opinion?"

"No. I'm asking you…out."

"Out?"

"Yeah." He shrugged. "Out."

She was deflated, and relieved, and disappointed, and still a little shaky, and thoroughly, utterly confused by his hot-and-cold, up-and-down routine. She didn't want to deal with any of his ambivalence—she was having enough trouble dealing with her own.

She glanced at her watch and started walking. "We've been through this before."

He fell into step beside her. "And I suppose we'll go through it again."

"I don't see the point." She shook her head. "Because there is no point to this."

"No, I don't suppose there is." He slipped his hands back into his pockets. "It's not like you're the perfect choice for a date."

Perfect. The word slithered under her skin and pricked at her temper. "Really," she drawled.

"Well, you do have your faults. We all do."

"Such as?"

"For one thing, your taste in hemlines leaves a lot to be desired." He shot her a quick grin. "Although last night's outfit was an improvement."

She stopped and stared at him, trying to decide whether she should be offended, or charmed, or amused, or vow never to speak to him again. Before she could make up her mind, he crooked an elbow at her, and she gave up trying to figure things out and slipped a hand through his arm so they could get going again.

"You know," he said, "I could give you a pair of scissors and a little fashion advice. Shorter hemlines could make your packing a lot easier the next time around."

"You're a real pal, Martelli."

"Yeah." He sighed. "That's me. Your *pal.*"

They walked in silence for another block.

"Are you going with Edward on the walking tour tonight?" she asked.

"I'm not sure." He steered them around a pile of Parisian dog excrement. "I'm ready for a break from the organized activities."

"What would you do instead?"

"Head up to Montmartre, have a quiet glass of wine in the artists' quarter."

"Sounds nice."

"It is. Very."

He glanced at her, and she thought he was about to say something more, but then he looked down the street, and the moment passed.

The next stretch of silence felt a little less comfortable, charged with something she couldn't put into words and the oddest feeling that they'd both missed out on something…important. "So," she said to break the tension, "you've been to Paris before, right?"

"Yeah. Years ago."

"Oh." She paused, waiting, but he didn't offer anything more.

They turned another corner, and there was their hotel, across the street.

Nick stopped and faced her. "A lifetime ago," he said.

"What? Oh, you mean—"

"Look, Syd—"

"Nick, I—"

They both stopped, stared, waited.

He cleared his throat. "Will you come with me tonight, after Edward's walk? To Montmartre? I promise…hell, I don't know what to—what to say or do. Just say you'll—"

"*Yes,*" she said, tossing aside her doubts and guilt

and common sense and surrendering at last to a crystal-clear impulse. "I'll come."

His grin spread into a dazzling smile that lit the dark corners of his face, and she felt as if she'd float away on the giddy bubble expanding in her chest. "Do you suppose Joe and Gracie can manage without us?" she asked.

"Oh, yeah," he said. "Something tells me they'll be shoving us out the door."

CHAPTER ELEVEN

AFTER THE TOUR dinner and twilight walk, Nick led Sydney to the nearest metro stop. He grabbed her hand as they jumped into the first train that *whooshed* to the platform, and he gripped a vertical bar and pulled her close as the car swung around the curves in the track. He couldn't get enough of touching her.

And all the light, casual contact had him aching for more. He breathed deeply, trying to steady the tight syncopation in his chest, and was lost again in the floral scent of her. God, he wanted her.

"This is our stop," he said as the train slid into Anvers. She looked up at him with that big, wide-eyed, Christmas-morning expression she usually saved for cathedrals and museums. His chest got all tight and hot, and then all those tight, hot sensations shifted to a lower spot.

"Come on," he said, a little too gruffly and took her hand again.

Faint carnival music drifted down the cobbled street as they climbed toward the pale dome of Sacré-Coeur. The aromas of marinated barbecued meats and fried sweets flavored the breeze. Hawkers spread cheap wares on tiny blanket squares, haranguing the tourists who edged around them.

He purchased tickets for the funiculaire and gelatos to help pass the time, and they settled on a bench to wait for the trip up the steepest part of the hill. Nearby, a group of preschool soccer stars kicked a ball against a retaining wall, arguing over tactics. He chuckled at the shouting match and then settled back with a resigned sigh when he noticed Sydney studying him.

"You understood what they were saying, didn't you?" she asked.

He tried to shrug away the topic. "Maybe."

"There's no 'maybe' about it." She delicately licked a drip from her cone, distracting him for a moment. "How do you know French so well?"

"The first two years in high school, I had this fantastic French teacher." He bit into his gelato. "I lived for that class. I planned on majoring in French in college."

"It's wonderful to have a teacher who can motivate you like that. How did he do it?"

"*She* had these incredibly long legs, and these incredibly short skirts." Nick tossed the rest of his cone to some tourist-dodging pigeons. "She always had time for tutoring during lunch. And I made sure I needed lots of help with my homework."

"I'll bet." Sydney narrowed her eyes at him. "But two years of high school French doesn't explain how well you seem to understand the language."

No, it didn't—but a guy didn't like to reveal all

his sordid secrets on a first date. Not that this was a date, exactly, though it sure felt like one.

"Look—here's our ride," he said, glad for an opportunity to change the subject. They squeezed into the crowded, stuffy train, and he pointed out landmarks as the car inched its way up the sharp incline. At the end of the short track, they followed the other passengers into the fresh evening air.

"Wait'll you see this." Nick led Sydney to a low stone wall, eager to give her something special to remember. He waved a hand at the panorama of Paris spread before them. "The best view in town."

"Oh, it's wonderful." She leaned against the edge, gazing over the rooftops of the city, and then turned to study the pristine exterior of Sacré-Coeur, fronted by deep banks of dark green lawn that flowed down to meet them. "It's perfect. Absolutely perfect, Nick. Thank you."

When she glanced at him with those wide, hazel eyes, he realized he'd made a memory for himself, too. "Can we go inside?" she asked.

"Of course." He tossed an arm around her shoulders in a casual move. "Come on."

He escorted her up the steps, past tourists enjoying the view and young Parisians enjoying the evening. She paused to read a plaque near the massive door, making him smile.

"It's so warm," she whispered as they crossed the threshold. "It's so much more alive, somehow, than the other churches we've seen. Don't you think?"

"I guess so." He looked around, trying to see

things as she did. Figures, silhouetted in candle glow, moved from one brilliant cluster of tapers to another, genuflected or knelt in prayer. The ghostly scent of incense hung in the air, and the drone of a Latin litany echoed from some chamber beyond screens of delicate wood tracery. "You're right," he murmured, "it is warm, somehow."

But she'd already left his side, wandering down a curving passageway. After dropping a few coins in an old metal box, she took up a long match and lit the end from another petitioner's candle.

He paused in the gloom beyond the bank of tiny wavering flames, watching her. Her eyes were sparks of silver, her hair shimmering gold around her pale, upturned face. Flickering shadow and light sculpted its lovely shape and played about the edges of her solemn expression as she lit a taper.

He longed to touch that face, to wrap her in his arms and draw her close. But this was more than simple physical attraction. He wanted to know what was going on in her head and what she was feeling in her heart. What she might come to think and feel about him.

He backed deeper into the shadows and shifted into storytelling mode, willing a scene to come to him in this inspirational place, for her magic to work on his imagination instead of his emotions. But she was more woman than muse to him tonight. A funny, inquisitive, difficult, sensitive, beautiful woman who inspired more than stories.

She turned to face him as he moved to her side.

"It's so strange," she said, "to leave a footstep, or a thought, or a lighted candle behind in a place like this. In all the places we've been to. It's like being a drop in the ocean. Tiny, and anonymous, but a part of the timelessness of it all."

He tangled his fingers through hers. Her hand was small, so small it would disappear if he wrapped his around it, but it was somehow a perfect fit. He concentrated on the smooth texture of her skin, the coolness of her palm, the fragile feel of her slender fingers. He focused on what he was feeling on the outside, because it was easier—and safer—to do that than to deal with what he was feeling on the inside—this strange sensation that was deeper than desire.

"Ready to go?" he asked.

She gently squeezed his fingers and nodded. "Yes."

They exited the church and joined the stream of tourists flowing down a side street into the heart of Montmartre.

SYDNEY SIPPED the last of her wine and set her glass on the tiny sidewalk table she shared with Nick. Inside the café, a trio limped through an uninspired jazz improvisation.

"I tell ya, buddy, jazz just isn't jazz when it's not played in the good ol' U-S-of-A," said the middle-aged music critic at the next table.

"Yeah." Nick shoved his glass to the side and reached into his pocket. "Makes you wonder how the French feel about the way we fry potatoes."

He tossed some crumpled euros on the table, rose from his seat and offered Sydney his hand. "We'd better head back."

With the working light gone for the day, the artists in the square folded away their chairs and easels. She paused to admire a display of small, simple street scenes pinned to a stall. Their owner narrowed his eyes, measuring her potential as a customer as he wrapped his brushes.

Nick leaned forward, setting his hands at her waist and his chin against the side of her forehead. "I like these," he said.

"Me, too."

"Which is your favorite?"

"This one," she said, pointing. "The one with the blue shutters and the shadow on the street. I wonder who's inside that dark window, looking out. And the colors are so soft. So warm."

"You're a lot like this watercolor," he said, and his breath tickled her ear. "Soft and warm."

His casual touches and clever words had her heart fluttering. Or maybe it was the evening and the wine. "Are you suggesting I'm a work of art?" she asked.

"Uh-huh. Impressionist." He straightened and showed her his profile. "How about me?"

"Hmm." She squinted. "Gothic, I think."

"Like a gargoyle on a cathedral roof?"

"No," she smiled. "Tall, and dark. And kind of mysterious."

"There are no mysteries about me."

She decided not to mention the tall tale he'd told

her about the bruises on his face or the way he'd ducked an explanation for why he spoke French like a native. Not to mention his secret source of income. Publishing a couple of short stories wouldn't provide enough to live on, let alone a trip to Europe. "Maybe so," she said, "but there are any number of facts I don't know about you."

"And you like your facts neat and organized." He grinned as he cocked his head to the side. "What do you want to know?"

"How you know French so well."

His smiled faded. "It's a long story."

"I have a long attention span."

"I was afraid of that." He frowned as he took her arm and led her up the street toward the church. "You know I've been to Europe before."

"On a tour like this?"

"No, on my own."

They moved into the grassy area in front of Sacré-Coeur. Nick found a spot on the wide white steps that was fairly private and pulled her down to sit with him. "You're not too cold, are you?" he asked, gently chafing her hands.

"No, it's perfect."

It really is, she thought. She tucked away a memory of avenues studded with jeweled hues of red and white, of monuments illuminated in mellow floodlights and the Eiffel Tower glittering in the distance. And the feel of Nick's solid frame pressed against her side. "Well, go on," she said.

He wrapped an arm around his knees, making a nest for his chin, and stared at the rooftops.

"I guess you could say I was indulging in an extended temper tantrum," he said at last. "I had a big pile of money saved up, and I quit my job and took off. I went to Italy first and then wound up here. The plan was to spend a couple of days, see a couple of sights and then move on. But I sort of lost my way and ended up staying a while. Months."

He glanced in her direction. "I talked to French people. A lot."

"Why did you quit your job?" she asked. "What made you leave home for so long?"

"What is it that usually makes a decent, hard-working, reasonably sane guy go completely off the deep end and pull a stunt like that?"

She shook her head.

"A woman."

"Oh."

"Yeah," he said. *"Oh."*

"So." She mirrored his pose and cradled her chin on her forearm, her face turned toward his. "What was it that made you stay here in Paris so long?"

"A woman."

"Ah."

"Yeah." He rolled his eyes. *"Ah."*

She smiled. "The same woman?"

"Nope."

He gazed at the city again. "I met the first woman near the end of our senior year of college. She was everything I'd told myself I wanted. We had the typical plans—the little white house, the big backyard, the kids, the dog, the chocolate chip cookies. The whole package. I was ready, I was willing. I was a sensitive man ready for a commitment and prepared to do half the household chores." He glanced at her. "A pretty valuable piece of merchandise, don't you think?"

She couldn't picture the Nick he was describing, but she nodded. "Definitely."

"Thank you." He sighed. "Well, first she said we should wait until I got a job. A good one. For the security, she said."

Sydney was sorry she'd asked. This tale was beginning to sound uncomfortably familiar. And Nick looked so disgusted—with himself, or with his story, she couldn't tell. "Hmm," she said.

"Yeah. *Hmm.*" He plucked at the grass beside the step. "Then she said we should wait until we had the down payment for the house saved up. Just to be practical."

"I guess that makes sense."

He gave her a dark look. "Then she added one more item. A promotion. A magic number she wanted to see my salary reach, so we could afford the kids right away. I was getting pretty impatient, you can imagine, but I was so in love with the idea of the thing—you know, the big picture—that I just kept plugging along, saving my pennies, making my own chocolate chip cookies."

He ran a hand through his hair. "And while I was plugging along, some guy who made twice the 'magic number' came along, and off she went. With him."

Sydney regretted asking him to dredge up the memories. Listening had dredged up too many of her own—of falling in love for the first time, of falling for her lover's dreams for their future and his promises of forever. Of being left behind when he'd taken a role in New York. "I'm sorry," she said.

"Don't be." He shrugged. "Now that I'm older and wiser, I realize I was more in love with all those big plans than I was with her. At the time, she just made the picture perfect. It was probably the best thing, in the long run, her leaving."

"And your trip?"

"I took all that money I'd saved and treated myself to a trip around the world. I was trying to cheer myself up—with a little booze, a few broads—and then I ran into a little snag."

"The second woman?"

"She was French." He shot one of his wolfish grins in her direction. "She taught me a lot about the language—among other things."

Sydney struggled to focus on the view instead of the image of Nick's French lessons. "What happened with the second woman?"

"Her family didn't like me, for all the obvious reasons, and in my relatively few completely sober moments, I had to agree with them. When my money began to run out, I really lost my charm. None of us minded much when I left." He sighed again. "Not a happy chapter."

She placed her hand on his knee. "Thank you for telling me."

"Sure." He tangled his fingers with hers. "Tomorrow night's feature is 'The Tale of the Dented Fender.' Stay tuned."

A corner of his mouth kicked up in one of his quick, casual grins. But his smile slowly faded, and his gaze dipped to her mouth before rising again to meet hers. She saw heat and desire—and something new that both fascinated and frightened her.

CHAPTER TWELVE

SYDNEY TRIED to tug her hand from his, but he gently tightened his grip.

"I've never seen eyes like yours," he said as he leaned closer. "They're full of colors, like two kaleidoscopes."

His voice rumbled through her, and his thumb stroked over her knuckles, and she was tipping toward him, helplessly caught up in his spell and the magic of the setting. "They're hazel," she whispered.

He cupped the back of her head. "Hmm?"

"Hazel." She swallowed. "My eyes are hazel."

"Mmm." His fingers combed through her hair, holding her helplessly in place with a fistful of curls. He lowered his head toward hers, and his stubbled jaw tickled along the side of her face, and his breath puffed warm and moist against the tender spot beneath her ear, and her chest squeezed so tight her pulse strained and stumbled, and she froze, waiting, for…something. For whatever might happen next.

"I bet I could study your eyes for a long, long time," he said, "and never see all the combinations."

His teeth closed over her earlobe, making her

shiver, and then his lips traced a featherlight path along her jaw. "Let me test my theory, Sydney," he murmured against her mouth. "Give me a chance."

A chance. So little to ask; so much to risk. She shouldn't have come to this place with Nick Martelli, shouldn't have settled in this spot with him, shouldn't be sitting so close to a man like this.

And yet she'd wanted this—this memory, this moment in Montmartre. She'd wanted to blend with the lovers surrounding them on the steps of Sacré-Coeur, to step into this impressionist canvas of Paris on a summer evening, to be a part of the beauty and the romance. A kiss from a handsome, mysterious man would make it all perfect.

Perfect.

His lips brushed softly, so softly against hers, once, twice, seeking permission for more, and then she floated into the scene and pressed against him, sliding into his arms, sinking into this fantasy of a romance, kissing a rogue from a storybook, taking her chance at a perfect moment to treasure forever.

The distant bleats and *whoosh* of the traffic faded, and the cool rustle of the evening breeze seemed to die away. All that mattered was the slick, warm caress of his lips over hers, the mild note of his cologne, the tangy trace of wine, the rumble of his groan.

He deepened the kiss, slowly, thoroughly, stealing through her illusion to rob her of breath and flood her with fire and scatter her thoughts and take her up, up, in a sparking, dizzying spiral, and down, down in a dark, mindless rush. His arm banded about her, crushing her against him, and his tongue swept into her mouth, and she fisted a hand in the fabric of his shirt, thrilled to find his heart hammering an echo to her own.

This was something beyond the pale, pastel perfection of any scene she could have imagined. The vibrant and vivid burst of sensation swept through her, taking control, taking her somewhere she'd never expected to go, somewhere she'd never been before, redefining her fantasies and blowing them to bits. She was lost, so lost, staggering, falling, wanting... wanting more.

When wanting edged toward need, she pulled unsteadily away. Eyes shut tight, she waited for the tornado inside to unwind and disappear. "Oh," she said.

He rested his head against hers, and the prickle of his chin on her forehead was sweetly intimate.

"Yeah," he said after a moment. *"Oh."*

Oh, dear.

THE LAST PERSON Harley wanted to see sitting at one of her booths in the Shoreline Casino Lounge was Hank Barlow. He and another guy in a pin-striped business suit had slipped into the dim, enclosed space a few moments ago, and already they were hunkered down and leaning in for a serious conversation. As she approached the table, she overheard Hank's buddy mention something about his ex-wife.

Terrific. A late-night bitch-bashing session,

the kind that were usually long on hassles and short on tips.

And she'd probably have to deal with Hank sticking his nose into her business, wondering what she was doing here. He was the kind of guy who couldn't leave things alone without poking and prodding and manipulating them until they met his satisfaction.

To top it all off, she'd have to deal with the flipping, flopping pressure in her chest whenever she looked his way and saw that long, lean form tucked into the narrow booth. Or whenever he looked her way, just like he was doing right now, glancing up at her with those deep set, long-lashed navy eyes. They widened at first when he recognized her, and then narrowed.

She flashed him her standard smile, the one that was friendly and welcoming but not too warm and inviting. The one she saved for male customers she thought might give her a bit of trouble. "Hey there. What can I get for you?"

He hesitated, frowning, and then shot a glance at his buddy across the booth.

She stifled an inward sigh and turned to face the other man. "So, what'll it be?" she asked. "If you want something to eat, we've got some nice appetizers on the menu."

Pinstripes gave her a wolfish once-over. "I'll just bet you do."

Hank shifted forward, moving into attack mode.

"Marriage?"

"Yeah."

She figured his philosophical mood had something to do with Sydney. And though she didn't feel right discussing this particular topic, he seemed to need to talk. "I don't know that they do," she said.

He shook his head. "I don't buy that. I think there are some people who just *know*."

She understood what he was getting at. She'd thought that too, at times. Some couples made it all look so easy. "Maybe some people just get luckier than others."

"It's *marriage*," he said. "It shouldn't be left to chance."

She huffed out an ironic laugh. "How can you sit here, so close to the land of the midnight wedding chapel, and make a statement like that?"

He shrugged and gave his glass another twist. She rose and edged out of the booth.

"When do you get off?" he asked.

A torrent of confusing emotions flooded through her—hope, guilt, anger, despair—each of them a reason to do her job, earn her pay and get out of own. To get far, far away from Hank Barlow and his roblems with her neighbor. "I'm a big girl. I can get yself home."

"I didn't mean to imply that you couldn't."

"Then what did you mean to imply?" She leveled and look at him and waited him out.

"Nothing," he said at last.

"That's what I thought." *Nothing*. That's exactly

She pressed the palm of her hand into his shoulder. *Down, boy.*

"Whoa," said Pinstripes. "What brought that on?"

Hank smoothed a hand over his tie and glared at his buddy.

"Guess Hank here was just acting the gentleman," said Harley.

"Hank?" His boothmate grinned.

She tilted her head and studied the man in question. "It fits."

"No," said Hank. "It doesn't."

"A Henry would never fight for a lady's honor," she said with a smile to lighten the mood. "But a Hank? Be still, my heart."

"The lady may have a point, Barlow." Pinstripes's grin widened. "But that doesn't explain how you knew he was a Hank in the first place."

"I'm a friend. Of Syd's," she added as she pulled a pad and pen from her pocket. She hoped the visual cue would get things back on track—she needed to take their drink order and move on.

"Syd. And Hank." Pinstripes's smile turned a little slimy at the edges. "I get it. You're the monosyllabic kid."

Harley settled her hand on Hank's shoulder again in a casual, precautionary gesture and resigned herself to losing the small tip. She beamed her brightest smile at the obnoxious guy across the booth. "Actually the monosyllabic nicknames are a convenience. Unless we were dealing with the Sino-Tibetan language group."

"Huh?"

"Of course," she continued, "the inflection inherent in certain dialectical derivatives can affect the quality of the intonation, aurally distorting the monosyllabic effect."

"Huh?"

"Nothing to worry about, hon," she told Pinstripes. "It's all geek to me, too. Now what can I get for you gentlemen?"

"Bushmills," said Hank. "Neat."

"Original or Black?"

"You've got both?"

"This is a classy establishment, Hank."

"I can tell." He smiled at her, and oh, my that was a very, *very* nice smile he'd been keeping to himself. "The waitresses have advanced degrees in linguistics," he added.

He ordered the more expensive label. She doubted Hank was normally that extravagant, but he was probably giving himself an excuse to leave her a bigger tip. Nice guy.

Pinstripes chose vodka and lime, and the two men stayed for another hour, one set of refills and plenty of discussion about Pinstripes's ex-wife. He was the first to leave, after fumbling through an apology and a request for her phone number. No sense in burning any bridges, especially when a guy was newly single.

Hank settled deeper in the booth, obviously waiting for a chance to talk. They both knew she'd have to swing by and check on him, so she decided

to get it over with and headed his way. "Can I get you anything else?" she asked.

"I want to know what you're doing here."

"My personal business isn't on tonight's menu."

"Let me assure you, my interest in your business is anything but personal."

She slipped her hands into her shallow apron pockets. "I'm working."

"Did you quit the casino?"

"No."

He frowned. "You work two jobs?"

She took a deep breath and tried not to resent his prying. "I've got bills, just like everyone else."

"I'm sorry," he said after a moment. "Abo Thompson."

She flicked a glance toward the empty seat on other side of the booth. "Your friend?"

"Not a friend. Not exactly." Hank turned hi in a circle. "We work in the same firm."

"Hmm."

"He's going through a rough time."

She checked the room. Things were s slid into the booth across from him. " some of it."

Hank's lips thinned in a disappro wife left him in the middle of a fi cruise. Just got off the boat and did

"Ouch."

He glanced at her and then "I wonder how anyone can ev to last."

what they had between them, and exactly the way things were going to stay.

She exited the booth and spent the next several minutes chatting with the handful of patrons lounging at the bar. When she glanced toward Hank's table, he was gone.

And he'd left her a fifty-dollar tip.

CHAPTER THIRTEEN

A CRUSTY ROLL and a cup of tea were all Sydney could stomach the morning after her sidetrip to Montmartre. Zack and Eric shared her table in the hotel's cheerful breakfast area, and she tried to make the appropriate responses to their conversation while furtively checking the room for Nick.

She wondered if he'd slip into the empty seat beside her. She wondered how she'd react, what he'd say, what might hover unspoken in the space between them. She hadn't yet decided how to play the scene. Blasé, but pleasant. Friendly, but lukewarm. Infatuated, with a hint of panic.

There was no denying it anymore—where Nick Martelli was concerned, she was a total mush case. Inside, outside, the industrial-strength, family-size serving of spineless goo.

"What's this gooey stuff?" Zack squinted suspiciously at the contents of a tiny foil packet.

"Some kind of cheese," said Eric. "I put it on my roll."

"Your croissant," said Sydney. "Go ahead, try something new."

"Whatever." Zack dropped the packet with a grimace and spooned up more cereal.

Sydney sighed and sipped her tea. The new things she'd discovered about Nick had surprised her. He may have had the role of charming rogue down cold, but he was also a man with a heart that could break and a mind that could dazzle. He'd even played a pretty good white knight, coming to her rescue. In some ways, he was very nearly perfect.

No. No, not that.

He wasn't perfect, not even close. He was a knock-about-Europe kind of guy, a guy who gotten knocked about right before he'd arrived. A guy with a knack for dealing with kids—probably because he was just a grown-up version of a kid himself.

What did any of it matter, anyway? Here she was, getting all mushy over someone who was only out for a good time—a good time that would end in a few days. It wasn't like anyone was talking marriage.

Marriage. Henry. Mother. Sydney's cup clattered onto the saucer as a familiar, suffocating sensation closed in on her. God, she was tired of her pathetic litany of guilt. She needed a change in routine, a change in outlook, a change in—

A change. Nick Martelli might not be marriage material, but he was perf—er, ideal for a fling. A short-term, no-strings-attached, preengagement, bachelorette party kind of a last fling. So to speak.

Maybe he wouldn't be interested. His kiss at her door last night had been light, brief and placed on her cheek. Maybe he'd changed his mind about her—if he'd been thinking about her in that same short-term, no-strings-attached way in the first place.

Oh, well, it didn't matter. She didn't care what he thought about her. Shouldn't care. Wouldn't give him another moment of her time. She bit into her roll to prove her latest insane impulse hadn't affected her appetite, and she choked on a crumb.

"You okay, Ms. Gordon?" Eric passed her a glass of water, and she nodded her thanks as her throat constricted and her eyes watered.

"Excuse me," she croaked when she could manage to get the words out, and then she stood and fled from the possibility of facing Nick over breakfast.

NICK REMEMBERED Versailles had been a mighty impressive address, and things hadn't changed. The aging limestone fronts, stained with a patina like fine antiques, projected wealth and stature. Ruthlessly clipped greenery edged the broad avenues. Everything was manicured to within an inch of its life, elegant to the point of caricature and very, very French.

The tour bus rolled to a stop near the immense square in front of the palace, and Sydney sprang into action. She herded the North Sierra students to the base of the statue of Louis XIV mounted on a proud bronze steed and posed them for a group shot. She counted heads as Edward gathered the tour group at a side entrance and then reviewed the morning's plans when he stepped inside to arrange for their site guide.

She pressed the palm of her hand into his shoulder. *Down, boy.*

"Whoa," said Pinstripes. "What brought that on?"

Hank smoothed a hand over his tie and glared at his buddy.

"Guess Hank here was just acting the gentleman," said Harley.

"Hank?" His boothmate grinned.

She tilted her head and studied the man in question. "It fits."

"No," said Hank. "It doesn't."

"A Henry would never fight for a lady's honor," she said with a smile to lighten the mood. "But a Hank? Be still, my heart."

"The lady may have a point, Barlow." Pinstripes's grin widened. "But that doesn't explain how you knew he was a Hank in the first place."

"I'm a friend. Of Syd's," she added as she pulled a pad and pen from her pocket. She hoped the visual cue would get things back on track—she needed to take their drink order and move on.

"Syd. And Hank." Pinstripes's smile turned a little slimy at the edges. "I get it. You're the monosyllabic kid."

Harley settled her hand on Hank's shoulder again in a casual, precautionary gesture and resigned herself to losing the small tip. She beamed her brightest smile at the obnoxious guy across the booth. "Actually the monosyllabic nicknames are a convenience. Unless we were dealing with the Sino-Tibetan language group."

"Huh?"

"Of course," she continued, "the inflection inherent in certain dialectical derivatives can affect the quality of the intonation, aurally distorting the monosyllabic effect."

"Huh?"

"Nothing to worry about, hon," she told Pinstripes. "It's all geek to me, too. Now what can I get for you gentlemen?"

"Bushmills," said Hank. "Neat."

"Original or Black?"

"You've got both?"

"This is a classy establishment, Hank."

"I can tell." He smiled at her, and oh, my that was a very, *very* nice smile he'd been keeping to himself. "The waitresses have advanced degrees in linguistics," he added.

He ordered the more expensive label. She doubted Hank was normally that extravagant, but he was probably giving himself an excuse to leave her a bigger tip. Nice guy.

Pinstripes chose vodka and lime, and the two men stayed for another hour, one set of refills and plenty of discussion about Pinstripes's ex-wife. He was the first to leave, after fumbling through an apology and a request for her phone number. No sense in burning any bridges, especially when a guy was newly single.

Hank settled deeper in the booth, obviously waiting for a chance to talk. They both knew she'd have to swing by and check on him, so she decided to get it over with and headed his way. "Can I get you anything else?" she asked.

"I want to know what you're doing here."

"My personal business isn't on tonight's menu."

"Let me assure you, my interest in your business is anything but personal."

She slipped her hands into her shallow apron pockets. "I'm working."

"Did you quit the casino?"

"No."

He frowned. "You work two jobs?"

She took a deep breath and tried not to resent his prying. "I've got bills, just like everyone else."

"I'm sorry," he said after a moment. "About Thompson."

She flicked a glance toward the empty seat on the other side of the booth. "Your friend?"

"Not a friend. Not exactly." Hank turned his glass in a circle. "We work in the same firm."

"Hmm."

"He's going through a rough time."

She checked the room. Things were slow, so she slid into the booth across from him. "I overheard some of it."

Hank's lips thinned in a disapproving line. "His wife left him in the middle of a fifth anniversary cruise. Just got off the boat and didn't get back on."

"Ouch."

He glanced at her and then stared at the glass. "I wonder how anyone can ever be sure it's going to last."

"Marriage?"

"Yeah."

She figured his philosophical mood had something to do with Sydney. And though she didn't feel right discussing this particular topic, he seemed to need to talk. "I don't know that they do," she said.

He shook his head. "I don't buy that. I think there are some people who just *know.*"

She understood what he was getting at. She'd thought that too, at times. Some couples made it all look so easy. "Maybe some people just get luckier than others."

"It's *marriage,*" he said. "It shouldn't be left to chance."

She huffed out an ironic laugh. "How can you sit here, so close to the land of the midnight wedding chapel, and make a statement like that?"

He shrugged and gave his glass another twist. She rose and edged out of the booth.

"When do you get off?" he asked.

A torrent of confusing emotions flooded through her—hope, guilt, anger, despair—each of them a reason to do her job, earn her pay and get out of town. To get far, far away from Hank Barlow and his problems with her neighbor. "I'm a big girl. I can get myself home."

"I didn't mean to imply that you couldn't."

"Then what did you mean to imply?" She leveled a bland look at him and waited him out.

"Nothing," he said at last.

"That's what I thought." *Nothing.* That's exactly

CHAPTER THIRTEEN

A CRUSTY ROLL and a cup of tea were all Sydney could stomach the morning after her sidetrip to Montmartre. Zack and Eric shared her table in the hotel's cheerful breakfast area, and she tried to make the appropriate responses to their conversation while furtively checking the room for Nick.

She wondered if he'd slip into the empty seat beside her. She wondered how she'd react, what he'd say, what might hover unspoken in the space between them. She hadn't yet decided how to play the scene. Blasé, but pleasant. Friendly, but lukewarm. Infatuated, with a hint of panic.

There was no denying it anymore—where Nick Martelli was concerned, she was a total mush case. Inside, outside, the industrial-strength, family-size serving of spineless goo.

"What's this gooey stuff?" Zack squinted suspiciously at the contents of a tiny foil packet.

"Some kind of cheese," said Eric. "I put it on my roll."

"Your croissant," said Sydney. "Go ahead, try something new."

what they had between them, and exactly the way things were going to stay.

She exited the booth and spent the next several minutes chatting with the handful of patrons lounging at the bar. When she glanced toward Hank's table, he was gone.

And he'd left her a fifty-dollar tip.

"Whatever." Zack dropped the packet with a grimace and spooned up more cereal.

Sydney sighed and sipped her tea. The new things she'd discovered about Nick had surprised her. He may have had the role of charming rogue down cold, but he was also a man with a heart that could break and a mind that could dazzle. He'd even played a pretty good white knight, coming to her rescue. In some ways, he was very nearly perfect.

No. No, not that.

He wasn't perfect, not even close. He was a knock-about-Europe kind of guy, a guy who gotten knocked about right before he'd arrived. A guy with a knack for dealing with kids—probably because he was just a grown-up version of a kid himself.

What did any of it matter, anyway? Here she was, getting all mushy over someone who was only out for a good time—a good time that would end in a few days. It wasn't like anyone was talking marriage.

Marriage. Henry. Mother. Sydney's cup clattered onto the saucer as a familiar, suffocating sensation closed in on her. God, she was tired of her pathetic litany of guilt. She needed a change in routine, a change in outlook, a change in—

A change. Nick Martelli might not be marriage material, but he was perf—er, ideal for a fling. A short-term, no-strings-attached, preengagement, bachelorette party kind of a last fling. So to speak.

Maybe he wouldn't be interested. His kiss at her door last night had been light, brief and placed on her cheek. Maybe he'd changed his mind about her—if he'd been thinking about her in that same short-term, no-strings-attached way in the first place.

Oh, well, it didn't matter. She didn't care what he thought about her. Shouldn't care. Wouldn't give him another moment of her time. She bit into her roll to prove her latest insane impulse hadn't affected her appetite, and she choked on a crumb.

"You okay, Ms. Gordon?" Eric passed her a glass of water, and she nodded her thanks as her throat constricted and her eyes watered.

"Excuse me," she croaked when she could manage to get the words out, and then she stood and fled from the possibility of facing Nick over breakfast.

NICK REMEMBERED Versailles had been a mighty impressive address, and things hadn't changed. The aging limestone fronts, stained with a patina like fine antiques, projected wealth and stature. Ruthlessly clipped greenery edged the broad avenues. Everything was manicured to within an inch of its life, elegant to the point of caricature and very, very French.

The tour bus rolled to a stop near the immense square in front of the palace, and Sydney sprang into action. She herded the North Sierra students to the base of the statue of Louis XIV mounted on a proud bronze steed and posed them for a group shot. She counted heads as Edward gathered the tour group at a side entrance and then reviewed the morning's plans when he stepped inside to arrange for their site guide.

Nick hung back a bit, watching Sydney as they were escorted through a series of fabulous rooms, each ornately decorated with classical scenes and immense oil paintings. He enjoyed the expressions that flickered over her face, and he smiled as she paged through her travel books, checking on the guide's stories.

He realized he wasn't looking for a story. He wasn't even looking for an angle. He was just... looking.

Looking—and wondering about that kiss the night before. Wondering if what he'd felt had been an illusion, the result of too much wine or too much setting or too many expectations after waiting too long to get his hands on her. Wondering what would happen if he got his hands on her again.

There was one way to find out.

Eventually they were ushered out the back, where Edward assigned a time and place to meet the bus. After a brief consultation, Gracie herded a few members of her group to the gift shop, while Sydney followed the others toward the formal gardens.

Nick jogged up behind her and took her hand. "Come with me."

She tried, without success, to pull free. "Where are we going?"

"Down there." He headed in the direction of the reflecting pool spreading toward the hazy horizon.

"There's an awful lot of 'down there' down there," she said. "And we have to meet the bus in twenty minutes."

"So hurry up."

When they reached the level at the foot of the final stairway, he ducked to the right, stepping off the main path and angling between a high screen of lattice work and shrubbery. Just as he'd figured, the palace had disappeared from view—and so had they.

"What are we doing here?" she asked.

"It'll come to you in a minute." He tugged her up against him and buried his face against the base of her neck. She was warm, and slightly salty, and smelled of the lavender hotel soap. "Mmm," he murmured as he kissed his way toward her jaw. "You're so sexy when you're touring."

She leaned out of range and took a deep breath. Her eyes were wide and dark and clouded with pleasure and confusion. "What are you doing?" she asked.

"You couldn't tell?" He slipped his arms around her waist and pulled her back. "Let me give you another hint."

She shoved him a few inches away. "That won't be necessary."

"Sorry, Syd, I couldn't help myself." He stepped in close and rested his forehead against hers. "If I promise to be good, can I have a kiss?"

"What?"

"Well, one for now." He brushed the tip of her nose with his. "While we're in Versailles."

"We're leaving in about fifteen minutes."

He lifted a hand to cradle the back of her head. "So let's get started."

"Nick." She pressed her hands against his shirt-front. "This has got to stop."

"Don't you like kissing me?"

"*No.* I mean, I do, but—"

"*Syd.* Honesty's not always the best policy, you know."

She frowned. "Maybe not in your world."

"How about in this one?" He pulled her tight against him and brushed a soft sample of a kiss to one corner of her mouth, and then the other, and then the tip of her nose and each eyelid. Delicious, everything, all of her.

She whimpered a tiny, mewling sound, and slid her hands up and around his neck, but he retreated, playing it out, teasing them both, letting the antici-pation build and shimmer between them until he thought he'd die if he didn't kiss her hard, and long, and *now.*

"Ready?" he whispered. He could feel her heart thudding against his shirtfront and wondered if she could feel his. No illusions here—not deep inside, where it counted.

"For what?" she asked.

"For the kiss."

Her lips tilted in a smile, and she flowed against him, her curves molding along his body and her quiet laughter vibrating through him. Everything inside him ached to wrap around her, to hold her and take her and keep her and—

"Cheater," she murmured against his mouth.

He had to think of some smart comeback, to put

some distance between them, because he was about to haul her up against him and scare them both with the kind of kiss that meant serious business.

Neither of them had any business getting serious, but he was already in so deep at this point the best he could hope for was some damage control. Whatever it was that had started in Montmartre last night was gaining mass and velocity and increasing in momentum at an alarming rate. He wasn't sure he could stop it, and right now it felt so good he wasn't sure he wanted to.

"I was just getting warmed up," he said. "Warming up doesn't count." He wound his fingers through her hair to watch it coil and twist and spring back to her shoulder. Copper and gold and silk. "Are you warmed up?"

She frowned. "I think it's time to start back."

He nodded and followed her toward the palace. "Where do we go after this?"

"Fontainebleau."

"Bet we can find some nooks and crannies there."

"Nooks and crannies?"

"For the kiss."

She rolled her eyes at him, and his heart nearly rolled over and played dead at her feet.

SYDNEY YAWNED as she trudged to her room the next morning. Edward had kept them out late with a visit to the Eiffel Tower and a walk along the Seine. And these early tour breakfasts were killers.

"Syd!" Gracie stepped into the hotel hallway, her

hand on the doorknob. "Wait'll you see this." She swung the door wide to reveal a huge bouquet of flowers on the desk.

"Oh, my." Sydney squeezed past her and reached for the note tucked among the blooms. *Oh, dear.*

"Nick came by just after you went down for breakfast." Gracie craned her neck to peek at the card. "You two must have had a good time the other night."

"Yes. Montmartre was wonderful." *Have dinner with me tonight, just the two of us. Nick.*

She leaned toward the arrangement and inhaled the honeyed scents of peonies, delphiniums and clouds of snowy phlox. "Oh, this is just gorgeous. How did he manage it?"

"I was wondering the same thing when he arrived. He must have been out shopping at the crack of dawn. How romantic." Gracie's shoulders rose and fell with a sigh as she leaned against the open door. "He could be out planning a serenade at this very moment."

Sydney groaned and sank on her bed. "Please, don't give him any ideas. And whatever you do, don't tell the students."

"Well, I'd better get going, or I won't get my breakfast." She backed into the hall and bumped into Nick. "Hi, Nick."

"Bye, Gracie."

He stepped into the room and closed the door, shutting her out. "That serenade idea's a pretty good one. I'm surprised I didn't think of it myself. Must be losing my touch."

"Any man who would give a woman a bouquet as beautiful as this one is definitely not losing his touch." Sydney stood to face him. "Thank you."

"You're impressed, I can tell." He closed the gap between them and ran the backs of his knuckles gently down her cheek. "You know, I could impress the hell out of you, if you'd give me half a chance."

She swallowed, dousing the lick of flame that followed his touch. "Don't you think I've given you 'half a chance' already?"

"It was the other half I was hoping for."

He grabbed her shirtfront, tugged her close and lowered his face to kissing range. "What about dinner?"

She shook her head. "I can't keep skipping out on my chaperoning duties."

"Mmm." His breath brushed over her lips, warm and moist and tantalizing. "Rain check?"

"I—I don't know."

He stared at her intently. "Figure it out, Syd."

She managed a tiny nod. "All right."

"Okay, then," he said. And then he released her and backed away. "It's a date."

CHAPTER FOURTEEN

SYDNEY SET her cafeteria selections on Gracie's table in the Louvre's dining area that afternoon and slid into her chair.

"What in the world is that stuff?" Joe asked, staring at the colorful items on her plates.

"I have no idea," said Sydney, "but I hope it tastes as good as it looks." She hadn't been able to eat a full meal since London, and she hoped the appetizing dishes on her tray would tempt her to try. Poking at a layered creation with her fork, she decided it might be a cousin to a quiche.

"What's in your glass?" Gracie pointed to her frothy yellow drink.

"Mostly fruit."

Joe picked up a French fry. "I'm glad Nick's been around to translate so I know what I'm putting in my mouth."

Sydney didn't think language problems would prevent Joe from grazing his way through France.

"Where is he?" asked Gracie.

"Nick?" Joe shoved the fry into his mouth. "Lauren and Heather pulled him into one of the shops downstairs. Souvenir advice."

"He's had a busy shopping day," said Gracie. "Nick?"

"He started this morning, with flowers for Syd." Sydney dropped her fork.

"Flowers?" Joe seemed truly and deeply shocked—the hand holding another fry halted before it reached his mouth.

"You should have seen them," said Gracie. "They were simply gorgeous—a huge bouquet. He brought them in during breakfast. Said he'd been spying in the hallway for his chance all morning." She sighed and leaned her chin in her hand. "Isn't it romantic?"

"Flowers?" Joe dropped the fry and stared at Sydney. "He brought you flowers?"

"You didn't know?" Gracie beamed. "Don't they make a handsome couple?"

"We're not a couple." Sydney set her napkin on her plate and shoved her tray to the side. She figured she'd regain her appetite when she got back to California.

SYDNEY JOINED several of her students near the inverted glass pyramid piercing the subterranean courtyard of the Louvre. Inside the glass, workers with suction cups attached to their feet leaned over structural bars, patiently washing and wiping each triangular pane.

"Nasty," said Zack.

"I know," said Matt. "Like, how dirty can it get inside that thing? The outside probably gets hit with pigeon shit and stuff, but why are they cleaning the inside?"

"It's like some torture my mom would think up," said Zack.

"Mine, too," said Sydney. "I'm glad she's not here to see this." Housekeeping chores—and Sydney's failure to do them—had long been a source of exasperation for her mother.

"What are we doing this afternoon?" asked Lori. "It's free time, right?"

"I think we should spend the rest of the day right here," said Sydney. "The hour we spent with Edward this morning wasn't enough to do this place justice."

"You mean, stay in this museum until dinnertime?" Zack looked appalled.

"But there's so much to see." Sydney pulled a guidebook from her tote. "Where's Mrs. Drew?"

"She went to the rest room," said Lori. "She said she'd meet us here in a couple of minutes."

"Is there anything else here besides art stuff?" asked Gina.

"Yes." Sydney flipped through the book, trying to find something that might appeal to the teen crowd. "There's lots of interesting things. Things like…um…"

"Ahem. Ms. Gordon." Nick's deep voice rumbled from behind her. "A word with you, please?"

He took her hand and pulled her toward one of the benches along the wall. When she heard teen whispering behind them, she tugged her hand free.

He turned and stared at her. "You're blushing."

"We've got an audience."

"You've got a problem with that?"

"When I'm not on stage, yes, I have a problem with that."

He glanced at the students and frowned. "Makes me tempted to rescind my offer before I've made it."

"What offer?"

"Joe wants to know if we can trade two of our I-want-to-stay-heres for all of your anywhere-but-a-museums."

"Deal," said Sydney. "And thanks."

"No problem." He shot her a look that made her mouth go dry. "But not exactly the afternoon I'd planned."

"Planned?" she managed to ask after a moment.

"That rain check, Sydney." He leaned in close, and her face heated again. "I plan to collect on it. And when I'm ready to collect on it, you'll damn well know it."

NICK RAISED his hand, signaling for silence as Joe shoved his way into their hotel room shortly before dinner that evening. "Just want to finish this scene."

Joe tossed his backpack on the floor, toed off his shoes and collapsed, facefirst, on his bed. "I can't believe I ate that last éclair."

"I can't believe you ate that second lunch," said Nick. He closed his laptop and then leaned to the side to open the narrow balcony window. Long sheer curtains billowed out against the iron railing, and the echoes of a soccer match in the street below drifted in.

"I heard about the flowers," said Joe. "Smooth move. Real romantic. Wait'll Connie hears about it."

"Why does she have to?"

"Are you suggesting I keep something from my wife?"

"There's nothing to tell. Therefore, nothing to hide." Nick sipped from the can of soda at his elbow.

"I get it. Payback," said Joe. He moaned and rolled to his side. "For the dare."

Nick shrugged and took another sip.

"You've never lost a dare before," said Joe.

"There was no dare."

"It was implied."

"Technically an implication doesn't count."

"Still," said Joe, "you've never lost before."

"Older. Wiser."

"Loser," said Joe.

Nick took a deep breath. "Funny. It doesn't feel that way, not from where I'm sitting."

"What does it feel like?"

Like I'm going down for the count. And going nowhere. She had a boyfriend—sort of. He had other plans. Together, they had all this…chemistry. But no time to run a couple of experiments to see what they might make of it.

"So," said Joe. "I won."

"Guess so." Nick slumped in the chair to brood for a minute. And then he decided that brooding about a woman who wasn't his, who never would be his, who he'd never see again after the tour ended, who wasn't even the kind of woman he usually brooded over in the first place, was pretty stupid. Almost as stupid as this discussion of the nonexistent stupid dare.

"It's no fun winning like this," said Joe.

"Like what?"

"By default."

"What do you mean, by default?"

"You're not even trying."

"I gave her flowers, for cryin' out loud."

"Forget it." Joe chopped a hand through the air. "Forget the damn dare. You win, okay? I give up."

"You never give up."

"Older. Wiser."

"Quitter," said Nick.

"I'm not a quitter."

"And I'm not a loser."

"So where do we stand?"

Nick took a deep breath and huffed it out. "On some pretty shaky ground."

"Is this the older and wiser part?"

"You mean, the fact that I can admit I don't have a clue what I'm doing?"

"Yeah," said Joe. "That would be it."

Nick stood and tossed his empty soda can into the tiny French trash bin.

"So," said Joe, "gonna ride it out?"

"Maybe." Nick looked at his brother and smiled. "For as long as I can keep my ass in the saddle."

CHAPTER FIFTEEN

THE REMAINING DAYS in Paris were like the scenes in one of the classic black-and-white movies Sydney loved to rent and cry over on weekends. Nick was attentive and always entertaining. And if he hadn't stolen another breath-robbing, sense-scrambling kiss, well, maybe that was for the best. It gave their time together a bittersweet, black-and-white effect.

They'd always have Paris.

He strolled with her through the Tuileries gardens and bought her espresso at a fashionable little café on the Champs-Élysées. He arranged an afternoon's bicycle ride for the students through the Bois de Boulogne and invented outrageous behind-the-scenes stories about the paintings in the Musée d'Orsay, coaxing them to examine the works of art with a little more care than they might have taken without the commentary.

Her first impressions of Nick Martelli had been all wrong. He wasn't an inappropriate tour chaperone—he was creative and unconventional and fun. He was…

Perfect.

TWO DAYS BEFORE Sydney was due to return, Henry opened his door to find Harley on his front porch. "What are you doing here?" he asked.

"Taking care of a little business."

He glanced at her too-blond-to-be-real hair done up in a pixie-on-acid style, and her neon-pink tank tucked into hip-hugging shorts, and the coordinating pink toenails fanning over dusty flip-flops, and he wondered for the hundredth time what it was about her that made his mouth water and his pulse pound and the guy below the border jump to attention. Maybe it was temporary insanity. Or maybe he'd come down with a case of extraordinarily bad taste.

He frowned at her, like he always did when he first saw her, and tried to decide whether to invite her in. It was probably a bad idea, but she'd made that trip to his office to return his glass—after filling him with coffee the day she'd found him at Norma's. Not to mention the fact that she'd sat at her kitchen table for over an hour that afternoon, listening to his problems. The least he could do was offer her a drink and five or ten minutes of his time. "Come in."

Her pretty mouth twisted in a lopsided, sarcastic grin. "Thanks. I thought you'd never ask."

He shifted aside and she strolled past him, her musky scent drifting into his nostrils and rushing through his bloodstream like a narcotic.

"Some place you've got here, Hank." She paused and tilted her head, staring at the craftsman revival chandelier suspended from the vaulted ceiling. Then she lowered her gaze and smiled at him, her friendly, before stepping inside. Pungent smoke blended with the odors of wine and colognes in a permanent inversion layer near the low ceiling, and the glowing ends of cigarettes and the flicker of table candles formed pinpricks of light in the hazy atmosphere. Coupled silhouettes moved like pendulums on the cramped dance floor.

Nick took her hand and navigated a path to a table near the dancers. He seated her in the one available chair and borrowed another after a heated discussion with a surly waiter. "Sorry," he said as he settled and slipped an arm along the back of her seat. "That'll probably delay our drink order by about half an hour."

She rested against his arm and felt his fingers tangling in the hair at her nape. He seemed different tonight. Quiet, moody. Reluctant to talk. She must have seemed the same, because she didn't know how to fill the silences between them. Too many emotions threatened to flood into the spaces, and she struggled for some safe, shallow topic.

The band began a teasing introduction to an old-fashioned tune. Nick leaned toward her, his jaw grazing the side of her neck. "Dance with me, Sydney."

He guided her into the midst of the swaying bodies and drew her hand to his mouth to brush a kiss over her knuckles before pressing her palm over his chest. She could feel his heart beating its own rhythm, out of sync with the seductive tones of the bass.

open, what-you-see-is-what-you-get smile, the one that always zinged right through his gut and made it hard to look away. "Nice, very nice. Prairie style, right?"

"Right."

"Always been a fan of Frank's."

"Frank?"

"Lloyd Wright."

Where did she come up with this stuff? He nodded and tried to remember why he should stay at least an arm's length away from her.

"Can't see Syd's stuff fitting in with the decor, though," she said.

Oh, right—Sydney. "You're right. It won't."

"You might have a fight on your hands. She loves her treasures."

"One person's treasures are another person's flea market rejects." He gestured toward the back of the house. "Want a drink? I've got soda, herbal tea, bottled water…"

"Hmm." She shook her head. "Tempting, but…no, I'd better not."

She pulled a fifty-dollar bill from her pocket. "I just dropped by to return this. Nothing personal."

He stared at it, his hands at his sides. "Why are you giving that to me?"

"Funny. I asked myself the same question when I saw it on your bar table the other night."

"It's your tip."

"Precisely what services did I render to deserve such a generous one?" She cocked her head to the side. "I'd really like to know, so I can keep offering them to all my customers in the future."

A bubbling brew of jealousy and anger and frustration and lust rolled through him. "What do you want me to do?" he asked. "Take it back?"

She stepped closer and waved the bill under his nose. "I want you to treat me like you'd treat anyone else. I want you to forget about what happened."

"You mean, forget I kissed you?"

She hesitated, and then tossed up her chin. "Yes."

"I can't."

"Why not?"

"Because I want to do it again."

"Oh." She gasped, and her eyes widened. "Why?"

"I have no idea."

"What if I told you I don't want you to kiss me?"

"I'd say you were lying."

"This is crazy." She stepped away and set the money on the small entry table. "You can't be doing this. We—you and I—can't be doing this. We can't even be thinking about doing this. Any of it."

"I know."

She glanced at him, and the look in her eyes, and the scent of her skin, and the sound of her voice, and the shape of her face and the paint on her toenails stole his breath.

"So why are we doing this?" she asked.

"Like I said," he answered, moving closer, "I have no idea."

"You aren't the kind of person who does things

like this." She held up her hands, palms out, to ward him off. "Especially without thinking them through."

"It seems as though we're both learning a lot of new and interesting things about me lately."

Harley backed toward the door, and he moved to cut off her exit, and then he hesitated, and she paused, and her big brown eyes lifted to meet his, and he got another whiff of her sex-straight-up perfume, and all his common sense blasted through his pores like the shock wave of a nuclear detonation.

The next semicoherent thought he managed to register, in the caveman portion of his brain stem, was that he'd twisted one hand through her silky hair, and cupped the other around the nicely rounded back of her shorts, and that his tongue was plunging into her mouth, and her pillowy tank top was shoving flat against his shirt front, and one of her long, bare legs was wrapping around his khakis.

And then there wasn't another thought, semicoherent or otherwise, for a long time.

WHEN NICK APPEARED at Sydney's hotel room shortly after curfew on the final tour evening and asked her to join him for a farewell drink, she accepted without hesitation. A drink—or two—seemed like an excellent idea.

He helped her into a cab and gave the driver directions to a club near the Sorbonne. "One of my old haunts," he told her with a rueful grin.

Wise now to the ways of European drinking establishments, she took a deep breath of fresh air open, what-you-see-is-what-you-get smile, the one that always zinged right through his gut and made it hard to look away. "Nice, very nice. Prairie style, right?"

"Right."

"Always been a fan of Frank's."

"Frank?"

"Lloyd Wright."

Where did she come up with this stuff? He nodded and tried to remember why he should stay at least an arm's length away from her.

"Can't see Syd's stuff fitting in with the decor, though," she said.

Oh, right—Sydney. "You're right. It won't."

"You might have a fight on your hands. She loves her treasures."

"One person's treasures are another person's flea market rejects." He gestured toward the back of the house. "Want a drink? I've got soda, herbal tea, bottled water…"

"Hmm." She shook her head. "Tempting, but…no, I'd better not."

She pulled a fifty-dollar bill from her pocket. "I just dropped by to return this. Nothing personal."

He stared at it, his hands at his sides. "Why are you giving that to me?"

"Funny. I asked myself the same question when I saw it on your bar table the other night."

"It's your tip."

"Precisely what services did I render to deserve such a generous one?" She cocked her head to the side. "I'd really like to know, so I can keep offering them to all my customers in the future."

A bubbling brew of jealousy and anger and frustration and lust rolled through him. "What do you want me to do?" he asked. "Take it back?"

She stepped closer and waved the bill under his nose. "I want you to treat me like you'd treat anyone else. I want you to forget about what happened."

"You mean, forget I kissed you?"

She hesitated, and then tossed up her chin. "Yes."

"I can't."

"Why not?"

"Because I want to do it again."

"Oh." She gasped, and her eyes widened. "Why?"

"I have no idea."

"What if I told you I don't want you to kiss me?"

"I'd say you were lying."

"This is crazy." She stepped away and set the money on the small entry table. "You can't be doing this. We—you and I—can't be doing this. We can't even be thinking about doing this. Any of it."

"I know."

She glanced at him, and the look in her eyes, and the scent of her skin, and the sound of her voice, and the shape of her face and the paint on her toenails stole his breath.

"So why are we doing this?" she asked.

"Like I said," he answered, moving closer, "I have no idea."

"You aren't the kind of person who does things

like this." She held up her hands, palms out, to ward him off. "Especially without thinking them through."

"It seems as though we're both learning a lot of new and interesting things about me lately."

Harley backed toward the door, and he moved to cut off her exit, and then he hesitated, and she paused, and her big brown eyes lifted to meet his, and he got another whiff of her sex-straight-up perfume, and all his common sense blasted through his pores like the shock wave of a nuclear detonation.

The next semicoherent thought he managed to register, in the caveman portion of his brain stem, was that he'd twisted one hand through her silky hair, and cupped the other around the nicely rounded back of her shorts, and that his tongue was plunging into her mouth, and her pillowy tank top was shoving flat against his shirt front, and one of her long, bare legs was wrapping around his khakis.

And then there wasn't another thought, semicoherent or otherwise, for a long time.

When Nick appeared at Sydney's hotel room shortly after curfew on the final tour evening and asked her to join him for a farewell drink, she accepted without hesitation. A drink—or two—seemed like an excellent idea.

He helped her into a cab and gave the driver directions to a club near the Sorbonne. "One of my old haunts," he told her with a rueful grin.

Wise now to the ways of European drinking establishments, she took a deep breath of fresh air before stepping inside. Pungent smoke blended with the odors of wine and colognes in a permanent inversion layer near the low ceiling, and the glowing ends of cigarettes and the flicker of table candles formed pinpricks of light in the hazy atmosphere. Coupled silhouettes moved like pendulums on the cramped dance floor.

Nick took her hand and navigated a path to a table near the dancers. He seated her in the one available chair and borrowed another after a heated discussion with a surly waiter. "Sorry," he said as he settled and slipped an arm along the back of her seat. "That'll probably delay our drink order by about half an hour."

She rested against his arm and felt his fingers tangling in the hair at her nape. He seemed different tonight. Quiet, moody. Reluctant to talk. She must have seemed the same, because she didn't know how to fill the silences between them. Too many emotions threatened to flood into the spaces, and she struggled for some safe, shallow topic.

The band began a teasing introduction to an old-fashioned tune. Nick leaned toward her, his jaw grazing the side of her neck. "Dance with me, Sydney."

He guided her into the midst of the swaying bodies and drew her hand to his mouth to brush a kiss over her knuckles before pressing her palm over his chest. She could feel his heart beating its own rhythm, out of sync with the seductive tones of the bass.

She turned her head, trying to catch her breath, and he grazed his lips along her neck, moving in a silky, teasing, nibbling path from the tingling spot behind her ear to the tip of her chin, and the heat of his touch penetrated and flowed through her, liquid and electric. She shifted against him, her unsteady legs trying to match his subtle glide. As the final notes of the music faded, he took her face in both his hands and forced her to meet his eyes—those impossibly dark, fiercely intent eyes—as her body stilled and her senses hummed and his mouth slowly, slowly descended toward hers. Yes. *Yes.*

More couples moved onto the floor, edging past them, and a jarring change in tempo signaled a change in mood. Nick frowned and stepped away, and she breathed in stale air and willed her heart to stop its hammering. He took her hand and led her back to their table, where they sipped the wine the waiter had delivered in their absence and stared at the dance floor instead of each other.

After another song, Nick set down his glass with a snap. "Syd."

"Yes?"

"Let's get out of here."

He stood, pulled a few euros from his wallet, dropped them on the table and extended his hand. She nodded and gave him hers. They threaded their way past the crowd at the bar and made their way into the cool of the evening and the shadows of the street.

They walked a long time, beneath the glow of graceful street lamps and the dripping greenery of balcony planters, past shuttered shops and darkened doorways and clumps of students and tourists. He slipped an arm around her shoulders, and she wrapped her arm around his waist, and she realized, again, how well they seemed to fit, how easily they fell into step with one another.

"Cold?" he asked.

"No," she said.

They started across Pont Neuf, the floodlit facade of Notre-Dame towering nearby. Snatches of conversation floated up from a tour boat moving leisurely beneath the bridge, and Nick stopped and leaned against the stone balustrade to watch its passage. Sydney turned to admire the outline of the Louvre on the opposite bank.

"What time does your flight leave tomorrow?" he asked.

"Two-fifteen. We're taking the bus at nine, with the others. Their flights are earlier, but we can eat lunch while we're waiting for ours." She wandered in a loitering circle, waiting for him to move, but he remained where he was, staring at some point upriver. She settled beside him and watched the evening breeze toss his hair over his forehead.

"When will you get home?" he asked.

"When will the plane touch down? Or when will I step through my front door?"

He straightened and faced her. "When will you step through your front door?"

"About eleven o'clock at night, I think."

"You'll be tired."

She nodded with a sigh. "It's a bit of a drive from the airport."

He stroked his hands up her arms to her shoulders. "Will someone be there, waiting for you?"

Henry. With his ring. "No."

"No dog? No cat, no goldfish?" He moved closer, his fingers brushing up her neck to gently frame her face.

"No, no one," she whispered. *Please. One last moment. One last memory.*

"Tell me about your front door, Sydney." His words seemed to brush over her face as his gaze drifted from her eyes to her lips.

"It's half of an old French door set. Glass panels, blue trim, lace cur—"

His mouth covered hers, hot and insistent, impatient for more. She opened to him, willing to give him everything he wanted and to take everything he had, to abandon herself to complete absorption in another person, to the giddy climb and the dizzying high, to the ragged, aching ride of glorious romance.

This was what she'd waited for; this was what she'd expected from him. Wanted from him. To be devoured, to be possessed. To be devastated. He didn't disappoint her.

His hands slid down, down over the curve of her shoulders, pausing to outline the swell of her breasts, and then his arms closed tight around her, dragging her against him while his mouth slanted over hers in a greedy, frantic, fevered assault. She grabbed handfuls of his thick, night-cooled hair, and arched her back, and pressed her hips against his, straining, seeking, craving more contact.

"Sydney." His voice was a rough growl against her neck. "Sweet, sweet Sydney." Once more his lips found hers, punishing, tormenting, and his tongue swept deeply into her mouth, shocking, demanding. On and on it went, the mindless pleasure, the desperate, reckless, violent rush. She sighed into him, and he groaned in a raw reply. His hands slid up to pull the pins from her hair, and then they fisted in it as it loosened to cascade down her back.

He backed against the railing, dragging her higher against him. She clung to him, lost in him, terrified that she couldn't trust her liquefied limbs to support her or her lungs to take in the air she needed, and thrilled that she didn't care. Her body betrayed her, even as her mind began a panicked struggle for control.

"Syd. *Syd.*" He eased his grip and raised his chin to rest it against her forehead. "I don't think I've been this frustrated since I was in high school."

She sighed and squeezed her eyes shut, grasping at the seconds slipping by, wanting just one more hour with him. But it was time to go back. Tomorrow they'd say a proper and public goodbye before she boarded a plane for home. No messy, painful denouement—just a simple and very final farewell.

She opened her eyes to stare at the lights dancing on the black ripples of the Seine. "We'd better get back. How far to the hotel from here?"

"Half a mile, maybe three-quarters."

"I don't mind the walk." She pulled away and pasted a smile on her face. "After all, it's my last night in Paris."

My last night in Paris. The words hovered in another long silence between them as they strolled toward their hotel. She filled in the blanks with thoughts of all the things that might be said, or done, or felt, if they'd had more time—and then she reminded herself to be relieved they hadn't.

CHAPTER SIXTEEN

THE STUDENTS and teachers from New Mexico and Illinois were the first to leave the tour the following morning, taking noon flights out of Charles de Gaulle. Sydney hugged her fellow chaperones and blinked back the sting of sentimental tears, agreeing to keep in touch but knowing it wasn't likely.

An hour later, the California group walked with the Philadelphia crowd to the security screening area. Joe accepted a piece of Juicy Fruit from Gracie, shyly kissed Sydney's cheek and then gave Nick a long, back-slapping hug before heading down a walkway toward the departure gates.

"Wish I could stay and visit a bit longer," said Nick, "but I've got to pick up my rental car and hit the road."

"You're not staying in Paris?" asked Gracie.

"Nope." He raked a hand through his hair in a distracted gesture, his eyes sweeping the crowded terminal. "Seen enough of this town to last me a while. Thought I'd head east, see where my mood takes me."

Off on another extended holiday. Sydney

wondered if he'd stop for a couple of days in another picturesque capital, hook up with another woman and pick up another language.

Gracie herded the North Sierra students into the security check line and turned to give Nick a hug. "Take care, Nick. Keep in touch and let us know how the writing career turns out."

"Don't worry. I'll be looking for customers." He gave her a smack on the cheek and waved as she followed the students.

"Well," said Sydney. She donned a bright smile as if it were a costume and readied herself for the final scene. "It's been…it's—"

"Wait a minute." Nick took her arm and drew her to a window overlooking the taxi stands. "I got you something. It's not a present, really, just something to read on the plane." He reached into his backpack and handed her a flat package wrapped in wrinkled tissue.

She folded back the edges to see a worn copy of a crime fiction magazine. "Is one of your stories in here?"

"Yeah."

"Is it autographed?"

He grinned. "You want me to?"

"Sure." She pulled a pen from her bulging tote. He scrawled something across a page near the back of the magazine and returned it.

And then he took her gently by the shoulders and gave her a brief, sweet kiss on the forehead. "Goodbye, Sydney."

Why did his tender touches always get to her more than the heat? She wouldn't cry, she wouldn't. She'd take her cue and play it light and friendly.

She laid a hand along his cheek. "Goodbye, Nick."

Before she could pull away, he lifted a hand and curled his fingers around hers. Slowly, reverently, he took her hand in both of his, brought it to his lips and pressed them, long and hard, against her open palm, his eyes squeezed tightly shut.

And then he turned and shoved his hands into his pockets as he walked away.

JACK BROGAN tossed the empty whiskey bottle aside and watched it shatter in a thousand glittering, lethal shards against the urine-stained back alley wall. Rats screeched and scurried past his stumbling feet as he wove in a drunken haze along—

Nick leaned on the horn of his tiny red Peugeot and cursed at a van hogging the passing lane.

Jack Brogan swallowed the thick brew of yak milk and tea, tossed his gear over his shoulder and headed out into the frigid, miserly light of a Tibetan dawn. His wizened, gap-toothed Sherpa guide promised him that today they'd reach the remote monastery where Jack would spend the remainder of his days in a search for enlightenment and—

Might as well give up. He was getting nowhere with this.

He passed a sign. Not nowhere, exactly. Saint-Ghislain. Belgium.

He pulled his car to the side of the road, igoring

the angry blast of a passing truck, and stared at a neat field of some kind of crop. Sydney would know what that green stuff was. She could probably tell him where to eat dinner and fill him in on the local history, too.

Sydney. God, how he missed her.

He slumped in his seat and closed his eyes, picturing her buckled into her narrow, high-backed seat, racing through the clouds while she read the story he'd given her. He wondered if she'd slip into a bookstore someday and look for another of his stories. He wanted to know what she would think of his work. He imagined himself knocking on that blue glass door with the lace curtain to find out. He thought of looking down into her changeable eyes when she opened it.

He pictured himself checking into a strange hotel, eating dinner without her sitting somewhere in the room. He imagined working on his laptop at his hotel desk, knowing he wasn't going to see her later. He thought of the next few days, arriving in a new city, exploring without having to wait for her to count her change or manage his schedule or check on everything to make sure it was where it should be.

He shifted in his seat and tried to drag his thoughts back to his plot, to fix the problems Jack was having dealing with the slender strawberry-blond agent in the London setting—the one whose fiancé had recently been fished out of the Thames, bloated and crab-eaten and stabbed through the heart with a *La Cage Aux Folles* letter opener.

Forget it. He'd finished for now with the problems of fictional plots and characters—his personal reality was in a much bigger mess. Sydney Gordon was more than a seemingly innocent femme fatale, a breathtakingly beautiful and tempting woman. She was a walking powder keg of passion. If she were some kind of sexual grenade, he'd have been honor-bound to take her down, to blanket her with his body and prevent the explosion from maiming the other males in the vicinity.

He scrubbed his hands over his face. Those were Jack's lines, not his. But he had to admit there was something about Sydney that tugged at his deepest desires. He thought he'd buried his old dreams of the house, the kids and the dog in the backyard so deeply that they were moldering beyond repair in his little graveyard of good intentions. But at some point during the last few days, he'd begun thinking again of chocolate chip cookies. Of waking to find silky red-gold hair curling across the neighboring pillow, of seeing Sydney's face at his kitchen table in the morning.

He opened his eyes and stared down the road, but all he saw was Sydney. He snorted, picturing her fumbling in that oversize purse, desperately hunting for the map she'd already dropped. He smiled, thinking about the way she'd wickedly mimicked the pompous little concierge at the Paris hotel. And then his smile faded and he swallowed, hard, re-membering the flare of heat and anticipation in her eyes as he lowered his mouth to hers in the garden at Versailles.

He'd warned himself about the dangers of playing with fire, and he hadn't played it safe. That was a definite singe he was feeling along the edges of his heart, and it hurt more than he'd expected. What really had him worried was the residual heat, the lingering sparks. He didn't want any flare-ups catching him off guard.

On the other hand, what was that old expression—fight fire with fire?

He started the car and pulled into the highway, heading back to Paris.

"OH, SHUT UP," Sydney moaned, reaching for the alarm on her bedside table. She groped through the litter on its surface for the source of the annoying ringing that had awakened her. It stopped and started again. Not the alarm. *The cell phone.*

She sat up and kicked her way out of her tangled sheets. "Hold on," she called, staggering across her room in the direction of the muffled noise. Fuzzily one-eyed, she stepped on something sharp and hobbled the rest of the way to her dining table. "Probably some stupid salesman," she grumbled as she flung aside mail and magazines, searching for the tiny phone.

There—beside a newspaper still rolled in its plastic wrap. "Hello," she snapped.

"Hey there. Did I catch you at a bad time?"

Henry. The sound of his voice flooded her with panic and guilt—and a sudden yearning for simple things and easy answers. She had so many feelings for him, she realized as she sank into a chair, and so many of those were the best feelings she'd ever had.

"What's wrong?" he asked. "Couldn't find the phone again?"

"Yeah. Sorry." She sighed and rubbed at the headache brewing between her eyes. He knew her so well. "I guess I'm still a little jet-lagged."

He paused. "It's good to hear your voice."

"Yours, too." And it was good—so, so good. Dear, sweet Henry. Always there for her. How could any woman not love a man like that? "It's been too long."

"A few days, anyway," he agreed. "I—things got busy here. I'm sorry. It's been too long for me, too."

She glanced at the temperamental cuckoo clock hanging by her porch door. The pendulum had stopped swinging. "What time is it?"

"Ten o'clock. I hoped that would be safe, for a Wednesday."

"You're right—it should be." For a normal person. She yawned and moved across the room to curl up on the sofa.

"I—I missed you, Sydney," he said.

"Same here." She wanted to change the topic, and she needed to set a time and place where they could meet and talk. Somewhere simple, somewhere public. "I think I'll head over to the theater this afternoon. I picked up some great ideas for finishing the interior set. London was an inspiration. Maybe you could stop by."

"Can't make it—got an appointment with a client." She heard Barbara's voice in the background.

"But I can hardly wait to hear all about it. How about dinner at the Inn? I could pick you up at seven-thirty."

Dinner at the Inn. The setting for his proposal. Sydney sucked in her breath. "Henry—"

"No pressure, Sydney—just dinner. It's been a long week, and I'm in the mood for some pleasant talk in a relaxed atmosphere." He paused again. "Come on, Sydney. Say 'yes.' Just this once."

She winced at his joke. She could handle pleasant talk and a meal in a relaxed atmosphere, and she owed him this much. "Yes."

"Great. I'll see you at seven-thirty, if not at the theater before that."

"Bye, Henry."

Yeah, right, she thought as she dropped the phone on a sofa cushion. She could handle an evening's date. Just like she'd handled one light, brief romantic fling in Paris. No strings attached, situations she could manage, feelings she could control. A definite end in sight. Just get on the plane and don't look back.

Only he had been the one who hadn't looked back.

To hell with Nick Martelli. To hell with him for being different than she thought he'd be. For all those sweet, unforgettable moments, for kissing her like she'd never been kissed before. And to hell with him for making her feel something she'd never felt before.

If this was jet lag, it was worse than the flu. She stared at the stack of newspapers and mail on her table and beyond that to the dirty dishes piled on the kitchen counter. Through a narrow opening she could see her suitcase lying open on her bedroom floor, its contents strewn over the edges. She'd hibernated through most of yesterday, telling herself she needed some rest after the long flight home. When she'd tried to interest herself in something fun—some sketches for the set—she'd failed even at that. Her one errand to the grocery store for supplies had gotten sidetracked, somehow, by a quick detour to the bookstore for another Jack Brogan story.

Jack Brogan, she smiled. Nick's alter ego—it was so plain to see. Even though Jack was blond, blue-eyed and generously muscled, he spoke in a slightly rougher version of Nick's own accent.

Particularly about women. Hook 'em up, reel 'em in, toss 'em back. If only she'd read the stories before she'd met the author, she might have spared herself a lot of grief.

Not that she was grieving.

Well, she was done now with thoughts of Nick Martelli. Completely and irreversibly done. Finished. *The End.*

NICK STARED at the sapphire waters of Lake Tahoe through his hotel window and let his mind drift with the faint, hypnotic trilling of the phone at his ear.

Connie's voice snapped him out of his jet-lagged fog. "Hello?"

He smiled at the sound of her voice. "Hiya, sis."

"Nick? Is that you? Where are you? Still in France?"

"Tahoe. California."

He leaned back in his chair and sipped room-service coffee during the long silence at the other end of the connection.

"You're not in Europe?"

"Nope."

"I'm sitting down now." A familiar dead-serious tone flattened Connie's voice. The tone that sent her kids and husband scattering in fear for their hides. "Tell me again where you are."

Nick pictured her in her sunny yellow kitchen, the counters smeared with peanut butter and jelly, the kids' artwork jumbled in a 3-D arrangement on the refrigerator. "Lake Tahoe. The California side."

"Joe told me you met a woman from California. Is that where you are?"

"Close."

"Ah, Nicky." She sniffed. "You know I've been waiting and waiting for this."

"Don't get blubbery on me, Connie." He slurped another dose of caffeine. "Is Joe up yet?"

"It's afternoon here, you know."

"So, how long has he been out of bed? Five minutes?"

She snorted. "Ten."

"Is he coherent?"

"Just, I think. Nick?" Her voice was suddenly filled with sisterly concern. "Nick?"

"What is it, darlin'?"

"Be careful, okay?"

Nick grinned at the request that sounded more like an order. "Anything for you, sis."

An early-morning breeze spread an extra layer of glitter across the expanse of water beyond the window. Close to shore, a sailboat's cupped canvas rose and fell over a speedboat's wake. The view was a jarring contrast to the soundtrack of crashes and children's voices raised in singsong teasing that assaulted his left ear.

"What's going on?" Joe's hoarse voice rose above the din. "Connie says you're not in Europe."

"I flew into San Francisco yesterday. Came up to see Lake Tahoe. God, it's gorgeous. You and Connie will have to bring the kids out here sometime and—"

"There's only one reason I can think of why you would be staring at Lake Tahoe instead of windmills right now." Joe sighed. "Answer my question, Nick. What's going on?"

Nick propped his feet on the windowsill. "It's the dare. You remember the dare, don't you, Joe?"

"I thought we'd agreed we were too old for that stuff."

"Romance, I think it was. Candy and flowers."

"I told you, I don't—"

"Did the flowers. Got the kiss. Collected that little item in Paris. Not that you ever bothered to check." Nick sipped at his cooling coffee. "Getting sloppy in your old age, Joe. And there is the little matter of a time limit. There's no statute of limitations on the terms of completion."

"You mean—you can't—are you talking about *candy?*"

"Right. The candy." Nick nodded with a grin. "But I'm working on it."

There was a long pause. "Are you *insane?*" asked Joe.

"Nope. Just taking care of business."

Nick heard Connie's murmurs in the background and Joe's shushing. Big brother was probably having a tough time waving her off.

"Have you seen her yet?"

"Nope," said Nick. "Gotta track her down, first. Piece of cake for a guy who writes detective stories."

"Just enjoying the scenery, huh?"

"So far. And trying to write."

"Trying?" Joe let out a low whistle. "This sounds serious, Nick."

"It is."

Joe sighed again. "What was the scene at the airport?"

"Pleasant. Light. Damn near impersonal."

"And you were expecting?"

"I don't know." Nick stood and paced at the end of the phone's cord, frustrated with the memory and on the defensive. "I keep asking myself why I should have expected anything at all."

"Yeah. All you did was try to show her a good time in Paris. Flowers, all that attention. She can't be expecting anything, either."

Nick stopped dead in his tracks and rubbed his

stubbled chin. "No, a woman would be crazy to expect a phone call or something after all that."

"Yeah, well, women are not renowned for their logic. Ouch!" Nick heard a small crash, and Joe swore under his breath. "Except for Connie, of course."

"I suppose I could have called her from Europe."

"Yep. You could have. Would that have solved your problem?"

Nick fell on his bed, raking his fingers through his hair. Discussing things with Joe was like getting his teeth cleaned—an unpleasant necessity. And just like an efficient hygienist, his brother always managed to poke into every soft pocket and scrape at the rough spots. "No. I've got to see her again."

"And you couldn't have waited another month, until you finished what you'd planned to do in Europe?"

Nick sucked in his breath. Saying it out loud would make it real. "I didn't want to stay there anymore. Not without Syd."

"Oh, hell."

"Yeah."

Another long silence stretched between them. "As your big brother," said Joe, "and the one partially responsible for getting you into this, I feel compelled to say something."

Nick grinned. "Is this the pep talk part?"

"Yep. Here it comes. Go get her, Nick."

CHAPTER SEVENTEEN

SYDNEY SMOOTHED a hand over the soft restaurant table linen. The candle flickering in a faceted globe, the spray of roses and baby's breath in a slender glass vase, the crisp Chardonnay in a delicate goblet—everything was elegant yet understated. Sort of like Henry's conversation so far this evening. Eloquent, but not overly verbose. Earnest, without being the least bit desperate. But mostly, his conversation was just plain understated—as in missing.

She grabbed her wine and took a long swallow. This facade of normality was driving her slowly insane. It was as if she hadn't left, hadn't traveled to another continent and reveled in impulsive urges until they'd nearly undone her. She wanted to confess, to throw herself at Henry's feet and beg for his mercy.

Or maybe another chance at a marriage proposal. Although she hadn't quite decided if she wanted one—or what she'd say if he offered it.

"Henry," she said, "we need to talk about what happened while I was in Europe."

He froze and studied her for a long moment, and

then he slowly lowered his glass to the table without taking a sip. "I can tell that whatever it is, it's upsetting you." He reached for her hand across the table. "I don't want you to be upset. We don't have to talk about it. We don't have to talk about anything that happened while you were gone. None of it. Not one word. Not if it's going to make you feel uncomfortable," he added.

All that repetition and heavy emphasis wasn't Henry's style. He was acting just the slightest bit *off* tonight. Still sweet, still patient, still understanding. Just not quite so enthused about it. Not his usual self, not at all.

It added to her own uneasiness about what she felt she had to say. "I think we should."

"All right." He sighed and gave her fingers a little squeeze before he released them, and then picked up his drink and took a long swallow of his own. "If you think it's that important."

She could tell from the oh-so-patient tone of his voice, and the oh-so-resigned look on his face that he didn't think it was. He was uncomfortable about the topic, too. But he was willing to go through the ordeal, for her.

He always made her feel so small and selfish when he took this tack. "No, it's not that important," she said.

He sighed again with what sounded like relief and refilled their glasses. "Are you sure?"

"Yes."

"Good. Good idea." He swallowed some more

wine and set his glass down with a decisive clunk. "Let's just put it behind us and forget it ever happened."

She couldn't believe he was brushing off her attempt to confess to an involvement with another man, that he didn't want to know every sordid detail. Not only because she was dying to get it off her chest, but because...because she wanted to see if he'd be jealous. He should be jealous, shouldn't he? Didn't he suspect what she was hinting at? Didn't he care enough to want to know for sure, to be just a little curious, to at least *try* to find out whether he *should* be jealous?

"Sydney." He took her hand in his again.

"Hmm?"

"I asked you to marry me before you left."

Here it was—the moment she'd expected and dreaded. The anticipation had felt like a kind of penance for her sins. And now the sad, serious tone in his voice and the mournful, resigned look on his face were a kind of punishment. She wanted to squeeze her eyes shut and hide, but she straightened and met his gaze. "Yes. You did."

He twisted his fingers through hers. They were long and slender fingers, artistic, gentle. She knew without looking that his wrists were dusted with fine gold hairs and his nails were perfectly groomed. His hands were big, and familiar, and reassuring. Not exciting, but wonderfully reassuring. Hands that would always be there for a woman. No matter what.

The man who owned these well-groomed, well-behaved hands would never leave a woman at the airport and walk out of her life forever.

She grabbed her thoughts and jerked them back to the topic at hand. She really shouldn't be thinking of Nick, not when Henry was about to propose again. It wasn't fair, and she wanted to be fair tonight. Fair to both of them.

"Henry," she said, "why did you ask me to marry you?"

"What do you mean?" He looked confused. "I mean, I don't understand what you're getting at."

She leaned forward and wrapped her other hand around his. She hoped she wouldn't hurt his feelings with her next questions. "Why did you let me go without pressing me for an answer?"

He seemed puzzled, at a loss for words. "Because patience is important in a relationship. And because, well, we belong together."

"We do?"

"Yes, Sydney." He nodded and smiled his perfectly straight smile. "We do."

"How can you tell?"

His smile faded a bit around the edges. "I—I just know."

"But how?"

"You're supposed to know these things. Especially before you make this kind of commitment." He picked up his wine and emptied half his glass. "And I do. I know. The moment I met you, I knew you were the perfect woman for me."

"But there has to be more than just knowing something, or feeling something in your gut." She leaned toward him. "Doesn't there have to be *more?*"

"Well…yes, I suppose. I suppose there's—" He shifted in his seat. "We also share many of the same interests."

She brightened. "Like the theater."

"There's that, yes. I do enjoy sharing that with you." He frowned again. "To a certain extent."

He didn't sound very convincing. She suspected one of those stuffy partners' wives had some doubts about her eccentric little "hobby" and had dropped a comment or two about Those People in the Theater. "What else?" she asked.

"We come from similar backgrounds. And we're both professional people. We share…" He hesitated, staring down at the table as if he were trying to find the right words. "Values. We have the same outlook on life. We're both serious people."

"Serious?" She wasn't sure she wanted to be described as *serious*. She certainly hadn't felt very *serious* during the past few days. Maybe he didn't know her as well as he thought he did.

Or maybe she should work on it. *Serious* had to be better than the impulsive way she'd been running—and nearly ruining—her life lately.

"Yes," he said. "Serious. About our lives. About our futures."

She snatched up her wine and swallowed a big, fat

swig. "Are we ever going to be not quite so serious? In the future, I mean."

"Yes." He nodded solemnly. "When we're having fun."

She wanted to ask Henry when they'd ever had any fun, any real fun, the kind of fun she'd had with Ni—in Europe, but she didn't think that would be fair, either. He was right. Their lives and futures were serious business. As was a marriage proposal. She should pay close attention and not be so critical.

"So," she said, "the reason you want to marry me is that we share so much in common?"

"It's not the only reason." He gazed out the window for a moment with a sentimental smile. "I admire you. I think you're warm, and friendly, and talented. You'll make an excellent hostess and a caring mother."

He shifted in his seat again and cleared his throat. "And I think you're beautiful, Sydney. The first time I saw you, I thought you were one of the most beautiful woman I'd ever seen."

"Henry." She was touched. He really was a wonderful man—and not just because he thought she was beautiful. "You've never told me that before."

"I should have." He reached across the table and waited for her to slide her hand back into his. "I realize now I've made a lot of mistakes, Sydney. I'll try harder not to make so many from now on."

Was that a hint of desperation she heard in his voice? It must have been her imagination. "So will I," she promised.

His hand closed tightly around hers. "And I do love you, Sydney. I do—I really do. For all those reasons."

"That's so good to hear." And it was.

"But why all the questions?" he asked with a frown. "I almost feel as if I'm taking some kind of test. As if you don't trust me, as if—"

"It's not that, it's—" She bit her lip. "Marriage is a big step."

"Of course it is. But don't you want to get married?" He cleared his throat. "I mean—"

"Yes, of course," she said. Eventually. Someday. "Of course I do."

"You do?" He sounded a little uncertain.

"Yes. I do."

"Oh." He stared down at their hands and then glanced back up at her. "Then won't you please say you'll marry me?"

She drew a big, fat dipperful of common sense and courage from that deep, deep well of affection she had for Henry Barlow. Affection like this could easily grow into an abiding love, she told herself.

And then she took a big breath, and opened her mouth…and hesitated. Just for a moment, but that's all it took for her life to pass before her eyes—and she didn't like what she saw.

But she had to say something. *Now.* "Maybe."

"Maybe?"

"No! I mean…not maybe. What I mean is…" *Oh, dear.* "I mean, I probably will," she said. "I'm definitely considering it. In fact," she added, smiling her most reassuring smile at him, "I'd like to wear your ring while I think about it, for just a while longer. If that's all right."

His face reddened, and he pulled his hand from hers. "I don't have it with me."

"You don't?"

"Not tonight."

"Oh." She was disappointed for a moment, but then a happy thought occurred to her: maybe they had more in common than she realized. "You mean, you didn't plan to ask me to marry you tonight? It just sort of popped out—like an impulse?"

"No."

"Are you sure?"

"Of course I'm sure."

Henry sounded upset with her. He'd never been upset with her before, even when she deserved it. He was in a very strange mood tonight—but then she was as reluctant to ask him what was bothering him as he'd been reluctant to ask her what was bothering her. All for the best, she supposed.

She reached across the table and patted his hand. "It's all right, Henry. It's going to be all right."

"I'm glad you think so," he said.

SYDNEY CARRIED two mugs of tea from her tiny kitchen the following afternoon and handed one to Gracie. She'd invited her former roommate over to discuss the post-tour cookie party they'd agreed to cohost at the high school in two days. Gracie had agreed that Meredith's idea was a good one—as long as Meredith kept her nose out of the planning stages.

"Here," said Sydney as she dragged a crumpled quilt to one side of the sofa and cleared a plump cushion. "The best seat in the house."

"The only seat." Gracie scanned the stacks of books, the overflowing baskets of craft supplies, the furniture refinishing project in one corner and the unmade bed visible beyond the bedroom door, and then shook her head with a sigh. "But don't go to any trouble on my account."

"No trouble." Sydney shoved a skein of yarn from the seat of her old wicker rocker and sat down. She'd tried to neaten her place, but she'd been spending a lot of time working on the set at the community theater. It was a good way to keep her mind off…things. "I was going to clean before Henry got here to take me out to dinner the other night, but I got sidetracked. What a mess."

"Your apartment? Or the date?"

Sydney stared at her tea for a while before answering. "Both."

Gracie sighed and shook her head. "I'm almost afraid to ask."

"Then don't."

"Then what will we talk about?"

"We're supposed to be talking about the post-tour party," said Sydney.

"If you insist." Gracie sipped her tea. "Although I don't mind listening if you'd like to tell me about this mess of yours."

"He said it was just dinner," said Sydney. "No pressure."

"And you believed him."

"Okay," said Sydney, "so I'm a sucker."

"You're not a sucker, honey. You're just too nice for your own good."

"Yep, that's me all right. *Nice*." Sydney got up and moved to the window and leaned a shoulder against the wall. She stared at the fir trees scattered around the driveway and the rocky shoulders of summer-bare mountains in the distance.

"There's nothing wrong with being a nice person, Syd."

"Well, last night I was too nice to say no."

Gracie choked on her tea. "What are you saying?"

"Henry asked me to marry him."

"And you said yes?"

"No."

Gracie set down her mug with a frown. "You just said you didn't say that."

"I didn't. I said 'maybe.'"

"Maybe?" Gracie sank back against the sofa cushions. *"Sydney.* You didn't."

"Don't look so horrified. I know 'maybe' sounds awful, but I did the right thing. I finally know what I want. I just need a little time to get used to the idea."

She took a fortifying sip of her tea. "You know, they say that a trip to Europe actually expands a person's horizons. You'll never be the same again, they say. Well, they were right."

"So, if you hadn't gone on the tour," said Gracie, "you might have stuck to your 'no' to Henry's first proposal and lived happily ever after?"

Sydney settled back in the rocker. "That's not fair."

"To Henry? Or to you?"

"That's just it." Sydney leaned forward, tipping the rocker precariously. "How would I know if I was living happily ever after or if I wasn't? I mean, what else do people expect when they make their plans? What do they do to make things turn out right? I never would have known that there could be…that things could be…"

"More?"

"Yes," said Sydney as she leaned back. "That's it exactly. *More.* Maybe what I feel for Henry right now isn't enough. Maybe marriage isn't going to fix that. But maybe I can make it enough. I want to fix it. I want to try. He deserves that."

She glanced at Gracie's doubtful expression. "He really is a very sweet man, you know."

"Yes, I know," said Gracie. "The male equivalent of a 'nice girl.'"

"What did you mean by that?"

"Just that you two were obviously made for each other." Gracie rolled her eyes. "It's so *nice* when a nice man and a nice woman get together. Everything is so…*nice.*"

"You make it sound like a disease."

"I didn't say there was anything wrong with it, did I? I said it was *nice,*" Gracie said in a syrupy-sweet voice, her expression innocent. "So much tidier than that messy opposites-attracting business."

"What would you prefer?" asked Sydney. "A scenario where a nice girl runs off with some smooth-talking, slick-looking, trouble-making rogue?"

"What rogue were you thinking of, specifically?"

Sydney's mouth opened and shut and opened again. "I didn't say me—I meant—I—it was a hypothetical situation."

Gracie stood and leaned over Sydney, her hands on her hips. "Don't you sit there all prim and proper and tell me about some so-called hypothetical situation. I was there, in London, watching you and Nick undressing each other with those two sets of ogle eyes. I was there, in Paris, watching the head-over-heels free fall, the rolling in the imaginary hay. I was sitting beside you on the plane ride home, watching you read that poor substitute for the real thing and mourning the loss of your 'nice girl' innocence like it was some kind of pseudovirginity."

She stopped to poke Sydney in the chest. "And don't you dare play like you don't know what in the hell I'm talking about, because I've seen you on the stage. You may be good, you may be damn good, but those rosy cheeks are a dead give away." She walked to the door and pulled her purse from the one hook remaining on the flea market hat stand. "Just answer two questions, Sydney Gordon. Number one, what makes you so sure Nick Martelli isn't one of the nicest men you'll ever meet in this lifetime?"

She opened the door and turned to face Sydney,

who sat frozen in place. "And number two, what makes you think a nice girl would be considering getting herself engaged to a man for whom she has no genuine feelings at all?"

The door clicked closed behind her, and the lace curtain billowed and settled back into place.

Sydney's face burned and her heart pounded. Gracie's words seemed to hang in the apartment, echoing in Sydney's mind. Slowly she pulled one foot up and tucked it in beneath her on the chair and then gently set the rocker in motion.

The cuckoo clock clicked and whirred, and the self-important bird raced out to bob on its perch in a strange pantomime. The mountain day slipped quickly into twilight, as was its habit, casting distorted shadows across the room. She sat in the gathering darkness, rocking, thinking, struggling to answer Gracie's questions, wondering if the answers were buried in feelings she was unwilling to confront.

Was Nick Martelli a nice man? She remembered her first negative impressions and how reluctantly she'd abandoned them as she surrendered to his charm. She'd been the last person on the tour to join his fan club, she thought, frowning. Why had she resisted so hard, for so long?

It was because she'd wanted to remain in control, and Nick had made her feel…not in control. Of the situation, of their conversations, of her feelings. His nimble mind and sense of fun, his sexual appeal had simply knocked the struts out from under her.

And he'd waged an overwhelmingly sensual, energetically focused campaign for her affection. A direct frontal assault. He hadn't frightened her away—she'd shied away and tried to shut down her very human, feminine response to his overt masculine interest. She'd been running from herself, from her own fears of making an impulsive mistake. Freezing her reactions, denying her desires, finding security in her almost-a-commitment to someone else.

Near-commitment. No commitment. She'd told herself she knew what she wanted, but then she was too afraid to take it when it was offered to her. Maybe the men in her life, like Henry, remained in her life because they didn't pressure her. They didn't make her pulse pound, they didn't make her heart twist, they didn't make her feel hot and panicky with a loss of control.

If Nick were here, in this darkened room with her, free from the restraints of the tour and placed dangerously within the context of her day-to-day reality, would she run in panic? Or would she surrender to her craving for his company and her addiction to his touch?

But he wasn't here. And he wouldn't be coming. She'd escaped involvement with the wrong kind of man, and she'd spared herself more stomach-churning qualms about out-of-control intimacy and a forever kind of commitment.

So why did she feel as if she were in mourning?

She rocked in the dark, keeping company with

her self-doubts and tamping down the lingering heat of desire—and dealing for the first time with the fact that she'd fallen at least halfway in love with Nick Martelli.

CHAPTER EIGHTEEN

SYDNEY SAT in the center of her sofa the next morning, comfortable in an oversize shirt, cutoffs and bare feet, using the pillows beside her and her locker trunk coffee table as organizing spaces for mail, magazines, important papers and junk. The next items on her agenda included starting a couple of loads of laundry and checking in with Gracie about the final details for tomorrow's party.

A thick, white pitcher hit the floor beside her feet and rolled to lodge against a ripple in the area rug. "Oh, Blackjack," she said as she stood to collect Norma's overweight cat from the recycled baker's rack she used for a bookshelf. He liked to prowl through her things when Norma was gone, and Sydney liked the company. "Good thing there wasn't any water in there." She frowned at the wilted flowers scattered over the floor and decided the mail would have to wait.

Her cell phone beeped as she carried Blackjack into the kitchen and she turned, concentrating on the sound, waiting for another clue to its location. The bedroom. She tossed the bulky cat on her bed and snatched the phone from under her pillow. "Hello."

"Good morning, my possible bride-to-be."

"Henry." He sounded much more cheerful this morning, nearly back to normal. "Hi."

"Busy?"

"Just getting organized." Blackjack jumped off the bed, scooted toward the door and then stopped and arched his back as a light rapping sounded on one of the panes of her glass door.

"Good idea," said Henry. "You want to—"

"Sorry, can't talk right now." She glanced out the narrow dormer window and saw an unfamiliar, expensive-looking sports car on the driveway below. "There's someone at my door."

"Call me back," he said. "There's something I need to tell you."

"Okay." The tapping grew more insistent. "Better run."

"Okay. See you later. Love you."

She paused, and he disconnected before she had time to respond. She hated when that happened.

Blackjack's tail bottle-brushed at another bout of knocking.

"Coming," she called as she stepped over the flowers and the pitcher and the ripples in the rug. She nudged the cat aside and opened the door.

Nick Martelli slouched against a porch post, his long frame angled across her landing. "Hi, Syd."

It took one moment for her to absorb the shock, another moment to register the emotional overload shorting out her thought processes, and no time at all to jump into his arms. She looped her arms around his neck and her legs around his middle, trying to get close, closer, and he staggered forward into her apartment, trying to maintain his balance.

Nick. She rained a flurry of kisses over his rugged, crooked, beautiful features. The familiar scent of his aftershave, the support of his wide shoulders, the strands of wavy hair brushing his shirt collar and tickling her nose—it all felt like a homecoming. And then the frantic pace of her welcome slowed, deepened and shifted in a heated response.

He twisted his fingers through her hair and pulled her mouth against his, hot and impatient and insistent, and raw desire surged through her. She reached behind him, trying to close the door, but her hand swung wild when he swayed, and she knocked a picture from the wall. The clattering frame startled Blackjack, who hissed and jumped on the sofa.

She threw her head back and dragged in a shuddering gulp of air as the room swirled, and he pressed his lips to her neck. "Syd, Syd." He moaned. "Oh, sweetheart, you taste so good."

"Up here," she demanded, and she grabbed two handfuls of thick black hair to tug his mouth back to hers. His tongue swept deep inside, and a satisfied purr vibrated in her throat. He risked another step inside but lurched awkwardly when his foot collided with an end table, and the lamp on its top tumbled to the floor. Blackjack growled, his tail lashing a needlepoint throw pillow.

She set one foot down, trying to provide more

support. His hand lowered to the leg still around his waist and massaged the back of her bare thigh. "Mmm, skin at last," he murmured, stroking his hand up to the hem of her shorts. She gasped and took his lower lip in her teeth.

He stumbled through another step, struggling toward the sofa, and slipped on the pitcher. His knee crumpled, and as they fell to the floor, her foot caught the edge of an ivy stand and knocked it over. The crash sent Blackjack out the door and yowling down the stairs.

"Are you okay?" Nick's dark eyes searched her face, and one side of his mouth curled up in his crooked grin.

"Yes," she murmured. *"Come here."* She grabbed the front of his shirt and pulled him down, and he shoved the locker trunk across the floor and stretched over her.

He was big, and heavy, and felt so good molded against her. Too good. She caught her breath on a little shudder of panic, the hard floor beneath her and the hard length of the man above her registering in some startled corner of her mind.

"There's something I need to tell you," she said.

"Mmm," he murmured against her jaw. His hand streaked up inside her shirt and closed over a breast. "Can it wait?"

"Oh." She arched against him with a sigh. "Well…"

"Sydney?" a familiar voice called from below.

Sydney closed her eyes and groaned. "Oh, no."

Nick's fingers slipped beneath her bra strap. "Who's that?"

"My mother."

His hand froze. "Is that what you wanted to tell me?"

Footsteps thumped on the stairs.

"No!" She shoved at him.

"Sydney?" The footsteps grew louder. "I thought I heard a crash. What's going on in there?"

"It's okay," Sydney called as she pushed Nick to the side and scrambled to her feet. "It's just me, being clumsy again."

She rushed to the door, combing her fingers through her hair and brushing her shirt down over her shorts. Her cheeks burned with the realization of what had nearly happened. What *had* happened. On the floor. With her door open and her mother a few feet away. With her new resolutions about Henry in tatters.

One touch from Nick and she'd completely lost control.

Meredith Gordon craned her neck to peek through the open door and check on things for herself. A pretty, petite blonde who shared Sydney's hazel eyes, she was always stylishly dressed and immaculately groomed, no matter the occasion. She cast a disapproving glance around the messy room with a sigh, and when her gaze settled on Sydney her lips thinned in annoyance.

Then she noticed Nick standing near the sofa, one shirttail hanging loose and his hair standing up in clumps. The summery warmth in the room seemed to shift to winter blizzard mode.

"Mother!" Sydney tugged on the hem of her shorts and took her mother's purse to hang on the hatrack. "What a surprise.. Did you just get into town?"

Meredith Gordon lived an hour's drive away, in one of the pretty little towns nestled in the Sierra foothills—a small pond where she could swim with the big fishes.

"I see I should have called before I made the trip. I'm sorry I disturbed—" She managed a small, tight smile for Nick. "Whatever it is I'm disturbing."

"Mother, this is Nick Martelli. I met him in Europe."

"How do you do?" said Meredith.

"Fine, thanks." Nick leaned across the locker trunk to extend his hand. Meredith hesitated, the merest fraction of a moment, and then slipped hers into it. He gave it a friendly, casual pump and flashed his crooked grin at her. "Glad to meet you, Mrs. Gordon."

Sydney took a deep, shaky breath. "I was just about to make some coffee. Would you like some, Nick? Mother?"

"None for me, thank you. I don't plan to stay for long," said Meredith. She removed a newspaper from the seat of one of the dining area chairs and dropped it beside a stack of books on the tabletop. "I have so many things to do. I thought I'd get a head start on plans for the wedding."

"The wedding?" Sydney laced her fingers together and squeezed. "What did Henry tell you?"

Meredith glanced at Nick. He shoved his hands into his pockets and returned her bland stare. "I'm sorry Henry spoiled the surprise," she said as she sat. "It's my fault, really. I called to discuss some financial matters—he's been helping me with that mutual fund, you know—and when he happened to mention he'd had dinner with you last night, well, I had to ask. He was very upset at spoiling the surprise—he'd planned on an announcement during a family dinner. What a dear, sweet man."

Her mother paused and stared at her, waiting for a response. "Yes," said Sydney, painfully aware of the still and silent man across the room. "He is."

Henry must have forgotten to mention the word "maybe" when he'd spoken with her mother—or maybe her mother's plans involved a way to turn the "maybe" into a "yes."

Sydney turned to face Nick. He stared at her with that carefully shuttered expression while waves of intensity radiated off him and slammed into her. "Coffee, Nick?"

A muscle rippled along his jaw. *"Coffee?"*

"Tea?"

"No, thank you."

"What is it you do, Nick?" asked Meredith.

"I'm a writer."

"Published?"

"Yes."

"Nick writes short stories," said Sydney. "They're very good."

He frowned at Sydney and tucked in his shirt. "I should go."

"No, wait, I—" She bit her lip. "We haven't had a chance to visit."

He cocked his head. "Is that what you want, Syd? A *visit?*"

She took a deep breath. "I want a chance to talk."

"Okay." He nodded, slowly. "That sounds like a good idea."

He glanced at her mother. "Good to meet you, Meredith. I'm sure we'll be seeing each other again, soon."

"We will?" Meredith's gaze strayed to Sydney, and Sydney could read everything that was going through her mother's mind. Another impulsive mistake. Snatching disaster from the mouth of success and security. Just like her father.

Nick nodded and gave her a cocky grin. "Count on it."

He shot another neutral look in Sydney's direction and walked to the door. The cuckoo chose that moment to spring out on its perch and bob with its silent scream. Nick scowled at the bird as he grabbed the doorknob. "That just about sums up the morning."

When Nick had gone, Meredith tapped her manicured nails on the table and gave Sydney the kind of look she used to give her right before she told her how long she'd be grounded. "What in the world are you doing?"

"I'm going to make some coffee." Sydney moved into the kitchen and slammed her way through her routine, and then she took a couple of extra-strength pain relievers. She didn't have a headache yet, but she figured one was on the way.

"Who was that man?" Meredith moved to the kitchen doorway. "And when was the last time you did the dishes? Just look at this place, Sydney. And look at *you*. You're a mess."

"I'm too tired for this discussion, Mother." Sydney leaned against her narrow counter and shoved a mess of curls out of her eyes. "I'm still worn-out from my trip, and I've got a lot on my mind."

"I certainly hope one of those things on your mind is your wedding."

"I need to get engaged before I can have a wedding," Sydney pointed out. "And I don't think that's going to happen. Not for a long time, anyway."

"Nonsense. You know Henry is perfect for you. Why you won't give that man the answer he deserves is—"

"I wasn't talking about Henry."

Meredith closed her eyes on a sigh. "I'm going to ask you again, and this time I want an answer. Who was that man?"

"Nick Martelli. I met him in Europe." Sydney poured steaming coffee into a mug. "Coffee?"

"No, thank you. You met someone from Truckee in Europe?"

"He doesn't live here. He's from—"

She froze with her mug halfway to her lips. She didn't know where Nick lived.

"What is he doing here?"

"He came to see me."

"I think you should report him," said Meredith. "He may be a stalker. He certainly looks like the criminal type—he looks like he's been in a fight."

"He's not a stalker. He's—"

How had he found her? She wasn't listed in the phone book. Had he called the school?

"*Sydney.*"

Too many times throughout her life she'd heard her mother say her name in just that way—with a world of disappointment wrapped around the hurt and resignation. It always meant one thing: end of the discussion.

Meredith turned and headed toward the front door. "I have to start back soon, and I'd like to get down to business."

Sydney set her coffee aside. "I don't know what Henry told you, but—"

"I'm sure he told me the truth—that you're still undecided about marrying him."

Sydney rubbed at her forehead and hoped the pain relievers would kick in soon. "Actually I've already decided that I won't. That I—I can't."

Meredith froze. "I see."

"No, I don't think you do." Sydney slumped into the rocker and sent it tipping back. "I'm just as upset as you are about this, believe me."

"I don't think so. Not this time." Meredith pulled

her purse from the hatrack. "You've disappointed me in the past, Sydney, but you've never made me doubt your sanity until this moment. I want you to promise me something."

"What's that?"

"I want you to promise you'll wait twenty-four hours before you talk to Henry about your decision." Meredith checked her hair in the little diamond-shaped mirror on the wall beside the hatrack. "And then I want you to use that time to think long and hard about how this decision of yours will affect your future—and Henry's."

She turned to face Sydney. "Will you do that for me? For Henry? For yourself?"

It seemed so little to ask in the midst of the chaos churning around and inside her. "Yes," said Sydney. "Yes, I will."

AFTERNOON ARRIVED with the glare of the sun through her sitting room window, aggravating the pounding in Sydney's head. Since she was already in a nasty mood, she decided it was an ideal time to attack the chores. With her laundry basket under one arm, she started down her apartment stairs to the service porch she shared with Norma.

Nick was waiting at the bottom step. "Hey, Syd."

Her breath caught at the sight of him, and some of the pain and frustration melted away. "Hey, Nick."

He started climbing. "Is there something you want to tell me? Something you were trying to tell me before we were interrupted this morning?"

"Yeah." She backed up the stairs. "I sort of got engaged. Not really engaged, actually, just…on a contingency basis, I guess. I said 'maybe.' To Henry. Henry Barlow. But I've—"

"Figured that might be it." Nick closed the gap and gently tugged the basket from her arms. "Why don't you invite me in?"

"Oh." That was a really bad idea, for all sorts of reasons. "Okay."

They stepped through the blue-paned door, and Nick set the basket on her table. "I want you to come out with me this afternoon," he said.

"What? Where?"

"You. Me. Out." He pointed to her window. "There. I'll wait while you get ready."

"Nick, I—I don't think—"

"For a visit." He shoved his hands into his pockets. "You said you wanted a visit."

"Yes, I did." She rubbed at her forehead. "All right."

He glanced at her clothes. "What you're wearing is fine. Especially the length of those pants. A definite improvement. And perfect for what I've got in mind. But you'll need some shoes. Sports shoes."

"Okay." She headed toward her bedroom. "I shouldn't stay out too long. I need to get in touch with Gracie. And now that Mother's in town, she'll want to check in with me about…about things. And I have to work on the set at the theater later."

He grinned. "I'd love to see it."

"Henry might be there."

Nick's grin got cockier, something she didn't think was possible.

"Henry doesn't worry me," he said.

CHAPTER NINETEEN

SYDNEY SLID into Nick's rental car, and he drove them to a marina on Lake Tahoe, where a sailboat lay waiting for them on a sandy slice of beach. Diamond-faceted ripples lapped beneath one end of the slight craft, sloshing against the curving white hull. Sydney stared at it doubtfully while Nick discussed some last-minute details with the rental manager.

"Okay, we're all set," Nick announced as he joined her on the beach.

"All set?" she asked. "Do you know how to sail this thing?"

"How tough can it be?" He shrugged. "It's only got one big sail."

"And another little one in front. Have you ever sailed before?"

"Nope." He grinned. "Come on, Syd. It can't be all that complicated. We push this in the water, we jump in, one of us takes this little rope over here and the other one steers."

She hesitated, staring suspiciously at the lines and the tiller. With a laugh, he picked her up and deposited her in the boat. The manager helped him shove the craft out into the water and then shouted more instructions.

"Did you hear that?" she asked.

"Don't worry about it," said Nick as the little boat bobbed farther from the beach. "So far, so good."

"Good. Great. Now what?"

"You take this," he suggested, snapping a line out of a toothy cleat and handing her the end. "I'll sit back here and play navigator."

Gingerly she tugged on the line attached to the jib. As she pulled in some of its slack, the rainbow-colored triangle of nylon above them grew taut and bowed. The narrow vessel seemed to leap in the water and head rapidly away from shore.

"Syd! You're a genius!" Nick adjusted the tiller. "I knew we could figure this out."

The boat bounced over a series of choppy swells that fanned behind passing skiers. She laughed and shook back the curls rioting around her face in the breeze. The dregs of her headache disappeared, and the tension of the past few days dissolved. "Turn more to the right to catch more wind," she called over her shoulder.

"Got it," he said with a grin.

Both sails flapped and puffed as he corrected their course, and then Nick found the right angle and they picked up more speed. He steered a course parallel to the shoreline, avoiding the traffic in the deeper water. The sounds of ski boat motors growled across the waves, and the scents of suntan oil and hot dogs on the grill drifted in the sun-warmed air. Sydney hugged her knees to her chest and laughed, just for the fun of it.

"Having a good time?" asked Nick.

"Yes." She shoved her hair back with one hand and smiled at him, but her smile faded as the situation—their situation—sank in. "I'm sorry, Nick, about…all this."

"Nothing to apologize for," he said with a shrug. "I'm just relieved you're glad to see me." He leaned toward her with a wolfish grin. "You are glad to see me, aren't you?"

"Yes," she said, because it was the truth. "I'm very glad to see you."

"Thought so." He made a slight adjustment to the tiller. "Your foreplay is a little rough, though."

Her cheeks warmed. "I wasn't expecting company."

"Bet you're popular with the delivery guys."

She watched the wind shove thick black hair over his forehead and plaster his shirt to the wide, square muscles of his chest, and her thoughts tangled with her body's reaction to him. She didn't know how much more of this she could bear. His sudden appearance in her daily life layered over her doubts about her future, and it all pressed in on her like a vise.

She also resented the questions her mother had planted in her mind, but now that they were there she needed the answers. She twisted her fingers together and squeezed. "What are you doing here, Nick? You should be somewhere in Holland by now, shouldn't you?"

"I changed my mind."

"And ended up here."

He grabbed a rope and removed it from its cleat. "Let's try turning this thing around."

After a few minutes of nautical mayhem, they managed to get their boat moving in the opposite direction.

"You didn't answer my question," she said. "Why are you here?"

He glanced at her. "I wanted to know what you thought of my story. The one I gave you before you got on the plane."

"You flew halfway around the world just to ask that?" She shook her head. "Wouldn't a phone call have worked?"

"I thought you were glad to see me."

She bit her lip and turned away. "I shouldn't be."

"Because you're somewhat engaged at the moment?"

"There is that, yes."

"And that's the difference between how you feel right now and how you seemed to feel a week ago? A ring?"

"Actually, I don't have a ring. Not yet."

"Actually, I prefer to skip the details." He shoved his hair out of his eyes. "I didn't bring you out here to talk about that."

"We need to talk about it."

"Okay," he said, his jaw set. "What exactly is it you want to tell me?"

She opened her mouth to say something, but the

first couple of somethings that came to mind didn't sound quite right. "I don't want to talk about it."

"Fine with me." He shrugged and tugged on a line. "Back to the first topic. What did you think of my story?"

"Actually I found it very interesting. Enlightening, even." She relaxed fractionally, though she knew the tough, important discussion had only been postponed. "First of all, the hero, this Jack Brogan."

"Yeah?" Nick settled against the hull, stretching his long legs over the narrow deck. "What about him?"

"What an arrogant, macho, reckless, irresponsible—"

"Some readers might find him self-confident. Virile. Brave and independent."

"Are you going to let me play critic or not?"

He narrowed his eyes. "It seems the role suits you a little too well."

She shook back her hair. "Secondly, the women."

"You find them enlightening, too?"

She rolled her eyes. "Especially that one in San Francisco. Full, pouting lips. Seductive, whiskey-toned voice. And a bosom that would register a 9.5 on the Richter scale every time it heaved."

Nick grinned. "Great line. Mind if I borrow it for my next book?"

"Seriously, Nick. Is this the kind of woman you find attractive?" She crossed her arms over her chest. "Makes me wonder what you could have possibly seen in me."

He adjusted the rudder and squinted against the glare of the sun on the water. "A world of difference, Sydney. That's the point. You're as beautiful as one of those quilts on your sofa and as fresh as one of the flowers in the garden beside your driveway. Besides, the women in those books aren't real, they're a...type. A certain style. And Jack Brogan, for all his good looks and brilliant intellect, is not me."

The sails slackened and slapped when the breeze shifted direction, and they worked together to set things right again. Sydney noticed the sun skimming the tops of the tallest fir trees, and her heart sank with the thought that this wonderful afternoon was rapidly slipping away. So much of her time with Nick had been measured in moments leading to goodbyes. This time, it would be much worse when he slipped away, too. And he would slip away, eventually.

Wouldn't he? "Nick?"

"Hmm?"

"Why does Jack Brogan dislike women so much?"

He frowned. "He likes women."

"Oh, he likes them all right," she said. "He likes them by the dozen. Likes them in tight-fitting clothes, likes them in bed. But it seems the ladies always get left in the lurch or sent to prison. Or just wind up dead. He doesn't trust them much, does he?"

"It's a literary device, a formula. Nothing personal."

"I didn't mean it as a remark on a personal level."

"Didn't take it that way." He grinned. "God, it's fun getting grilled like this."

"We could find something else to talk about." She fiddled with the jib and glanced at him over her shoulder. "We could talk about you."

He shrugged. "One of my favorite topics."

She took a deep breath and prepared to walk through the conversational opening he'd just provided. "We could talk about what you do when you're not writing. You know, you never told me what job you were doing before you went to Europe."

He narrowed his eyes slightly and studied her for several long, tense seconds. "I built houses."

"You're a carpenter?"

"Not exactly."

She waited, but he didn't volunteer any more information. "So what did you do, exactly?"

He watched a skier swoop by in a spray of water and turned the boat toward the wake. "I started a company. Specialty construction. We renovated old commercial structures for homes. Architectural salvaging of sorts."

"Sounds impressive."

"Sounds more impressive than it is." He looked down at his hands. "Was."

"Was?"

"I quit."

"Your own company?" she asked. "What did you do—sell it?"

"No. I handed it over to one of my assistants."

"When was this?"

"A couple of months ago."

"Right before the tour."

"Yeah." He shrugged. "I had a bunch of money saved up, and I decided to treat myself to another trip. Not all the way around the world this time, but far enough to get some good story ideas. To take a chance to do what I'd always wanted to do."

"To write."

"Yeah." One side of his mouth kicked up in a soft smile. "To write."

The financial risks he was taking shocked her. "You simply tossed aside a successful business for a chance like that?"

He shrugged and settled back again. "I was ready for a change."

"But what will you do in the meantime?"

"I won't starve," he said with one of his cocky grins. "Not for a while, anyway."

She shook her head in amazement. "And yet you spent a chunk of money on a plane ticket to come here."

"Another gamble. Makes me feel right at home with the other high rollers around here."

She narrowed her eyes at him. There was something—a whole lot of somethings—he wasn't telling her, she was sure of it. "Why are you here, Nick?"

His gaze drifted to her mouth, and his expression set off firecrackers in her system. "I thought you were happy to see me."

"I am."

"Come here." He patted a spot on the low bench beside him.

She scooted along the edge, and when she was close enough for him to reach, he took her hand and lifted it to his lips. "Reason enough for us both, okay?"

She nodded and gazed over the water. She couldn't look at him, not right now. Looking at Nick made her chest squeeze with delight and frustration and longing and lust—and it squeezed every bit of her common sense out through her pores. She was hours away from turning down a marriage proposal from a man who would never, ever consider—not for one moment—gambling his future on a trip to Europe and the slim chance of selling a novel he hadn't written yet. And she knew, deep in her giddy, greedy, wildly beating heart that she was hours away from jumping into an affair with a man who splurged on the price of a trans-Atlantic ticket to satisfy his whims.

"How about playing tour guide while I'm here?" he said. "You seem to enjoy it."

She flicked a sideways glance in his direction. "I have a lot of work to do on the set during the next few days. In fact, I should probably head back pretty soon."

"No trouble. I'm flexible." He fussed with the tiller as the late-afternoon wind kicked up. "We'll work around your schedule. Whatever you want, Sydney. Whenever you're ready. I'm not going anywhere."

Somehow his casual words sounded like a threat.

NICK HID A SMILE as he watched Sydney try to disguise the fact that he confused her. She wasn't very good at it, and he intended to confuse the hell out of her over the next few days. It would be so easy it would almost take the fun out of it. Almost. She'd tried playing hard-to-get with him in Europe. She wasn't very good at that, either. Besides, now he knew all her moves.

He'd enjoyed watching her moves this afternoon—the feminine muscles in her arms straining in her tug-of-war with the sail, her teeth sinking into her lip in concentration, her smoky hazel eyes squinting with effort as she experimented with the tension in the sail, the way her long, satiny legs disappeared in a series of interesting curves beneath the ragged hem of her denim shorts.

He'd take her sailing again, soon. Maybe he'd buy a boat of his own, if he decided to stick around for a while.

He aimed for the marina, and they came up fast on the shore. The manager raced out to greet them, waving his arms and shouting something. A passing speedboat drowned out his words.

"What's he saying, Nick?"

"Something about some board—"

The small keel caught in the shallows near the beach, and the sudden, twisting stop pitched them both into the icy water.

CHAPTER TWENTY

NICK HELPED Sydney stagger to the sand, where she collapsed with a sputtering laugh. "Boy, aren't we the best sailors ever?" She toed off her shoes and poured a small waterfall from her canvas purse.

By the time he'd helped the manager drag the little craft out of the water, her lower lip was quivering from the cold. "Come on, let's get you warmed up." He draped an arm around her shoulders, pulled her tight against his side and gently chafed her arm as they headed back to his car.

He settled her into her seat and jogged around to open his own door, and then quickly started the engine and stabbed at the buttons for heat and blowers.

"This is a first," she said. "Ski weather climate control in July." She tilted her head against the leather, shutting her eyes.

Nick stole a few glances her way as he waited his turn to pull into the sluggish, summer-thick tourist traffic, waiting for her chills to dissipate. "Sorry, Syd."

"For what?" She smiled and turned to face him. "That was fantastic!"

He shot her a disbelieving glance, but she ignored his reaction. Instead, she launched into a chatty monologue as he inched along the two-lane highway, entertaining him with tales of runaway river rafts, balky canoes and other personal disasters on the water. He limited his contributions to encouraging smiles while enjoying the glimpses of reddish hair curling in loose ringlets around her face and the way her voice wrapped around a memory and amplified it. He wanted nothing more at that moment than to listen to her talk and to watch the emotions behind her stories flit across her expressive face.

She was captivating, and great company, and he loved being with her. He loved the way she tried so hard to do things right but usually made a mess in the end. He loved the way her long, slender limbs moved in that graceful, feminine sway. He loved the way her mind worked and the way she rolled her eyes at his barbs and teased him right back.

He loved her.

Strange how that fact should slip under his guard and smack him square between the eyes at this particular moment.

And now he was certain he'd done the right thing coming here. That he'd done the right thing agreeing—sort of—to Joe's stupid dare, the right thing romancing her, courting her, kissing her the first time and every time since. And he vowed, as he slowed for traffic, that he'd keep on doing the right thing. He'd keep on romancing her, and courting her, and kissing her, until she agreed to marry him. He'd do whatever it took to bind her to him forever.

He had no doubt that Sydney Gordon was the right woman for him. Now he had to convince her he was the right man for her.

They turned into the wide driveway of a tall, starkly modern luxury hotel on the waterfront. Nick wheeled into a spot near the entrance and killed the engine.

"What are we doing here?" she asked.

"This is where I'm staying," he answered. "I figure we can dry off here, order room service and get you back home in plenty of time to do all those things you've got to do."

She stared at the hotel entrance. "I don't think this is a good idea."

"Because it'll take too long?"

"Because...*because*." She plucked at her wet shirt. "And because of this."

He climbed out, walked to her door, hauled her out and took her hand. "Come on, Syd. We'll pretend the wet look is the latest style. Think you can handle it?"

"No problem," she said. She shot him a sideways glance. "I've survived worse lobby scenes than this one."

SYDNEY STEPPED through Nick's hotel bathroom door a half an hour later, toweling her damp hair. He stood at the window in his jeans, barefoot and barechested, studying the view with a frown. She stopped and slowly lowered the towel. His sleek, muscular form took her breath away.

"It all looks so simple from here," he said. "Smooth sails just gliding across the surface. How hard can it be? And I thought we were getting the hang of it...until the end."

She smiled and folded back the huge cuffs of his navy velour robe. "How long did they say it would take to wash and dry our things?"

"About an hour." He handed her a room service menu. "I'll let you order for us both." He paused to brush his lips lightly over hers as he headed toward the bathroom. "I won't be long," he said, and then he closed the door behind him.

She pulled her cell phone from her soggy bag and gave it another try. Still dead. She wondered if it would come back to life when it dried.

She set it on the desk and picked up the room phone to call her apartment and check her messages. Nothing from her mother. Nothing from Henry. She thought about calling them, too, but decided against it. What would she say if she reached them?

She phoned room service next and asked for hamburgers, fries and soft drinks. Too bad she couldn't keep her life as uncomplicated as the menu. She was acutely aware of Nick's scent on his robe and her nakedness beneath the soft, weighty fabric. Anticipation swirled through her, setting every nerve ending tingling with energy. An hour to spend in his hotel room. An hour alone, just the two of them, suspended temporarily in a strange isolation from the world outside. No tour schedules, no curfews, no responsibilities to dozens of other people.

A week ago, she would have given anything for an opportunity exactly like this. Now she was terrified, trembling inside and out. Because she cared more for Nick than she had last week. Because she had less control over her feelings than she'd had last week. Because she was about to throw away any chance she'd ever have with a perfect man who'd told her he loved her in exchange for a chancy relationship with a man who'd never even hinted he could.

Stupid. Weak. And all she could think of was what might happen this afternoon and how to hold it close to her heart for the rest of her life.

Add selfish to the list.

And restless. She paced a circuit of the room and ended up back where she'd started, staring at Nick's laptop on the desk. She ran her fingers lightly over the case and recalled passages from the story she'd read on the plane. Phrases alive with his humor, the plot twisting and racing with his energy.

"What is it, Syd?"

She turned, startled. She hadn't heard him come into the room behind her. He leaned against the doorway, his arms folded across a broad, bare chest fanned with glistening black hair. A white hotel towel was fastened around his lean waist. When his mouth tipped up slowly in one corner, she ordered herself to stop staring. To stop drooling. "I was just thinking of Jack Brogan," she said.

"Should I prepare for another session with the critic from hell?"

She rolled her eyes. "I wasn't that bad."

"Everyone's entitled to an opinion."

"Isn't that the point?"

He straightened away from the door and adjusted the towel at his waist. "I've been sitting here in this room or driving the roads along the lake, reminding myself that I'm a writer, that I should be able to come up with something to—" He shoved an impatient hand through his wet hair. "I keep telling myself that I should be able to find the right words to get us to where I want us to be."

Where I want us to be. She was almost afraid to hope, but he was a writer talking about words—he must have meant the ones he'd just used. "Us?"

"Yes, Syd. *Us.*" He met her gaze. "It's time to collect on that rain check."

"That—" A shimmery thrill raced up her spine. "I thought that was for dinner."

"We'll eat later." He frowned. "The thing is, I've never had a case of writer's block this bad."

The rain check. *Us.* "You're doing okay so far."

"Don't start going easy on me now," he said with a tiny twist of a grin. He took a step in her direction. "I'm trying to create a story here. Beginning, middle and end."

She nodded, unwilling to speak, afraid she might ruin the plot. She realized she was holding her breath, waiting for him to finish his tale and reach the part where they could live happily ever after.

He took another step toward her and stopped. "I need you to meet me halfway."

Heart pounding, she ordered herself to put one foot in front of another until she stood before him. His lashes, still damp from his shower, formed long black spikes rimming his eyes. The smudges of his bruises were nearly gone, and the cut over his lip was a pale line. With nothing to distract from the strong, angular lines and bold arcs of his features, he was devastatingly handsome.

"I've never written a play," he said, "but I could try. We could make it a collaboration." He leaned forward, until his face was only inches from hers. "What does the heroine want?"

Sydney's pulse thundered in her ears. "I—I thought you were the writer."

"Ah, but I'm new at this, Sydney. I think I'm going to need a little help from a theatrical professional to get the timing right." He moved fractionally, his lips disconcertingly near. "It seems to me the timing's the toughest part."

"Yes. It can be." Hers certainly left a lot to be desired.

He fingered the collar of the robe she wore, and she gasped when his knuckles grazed the fabric covering her breast. "What about motivation?" he asked. "What does the heroine want?"

The look on his face scrambled her thoughts, and she closed her eyes to shut him out. But then his scent, warm male and hotel soap, filled her senses. "I can't think when you're so close like this, I—"

He took her arms and tugged her still closer. "What do you want, Sydney?"

"I want you."

His mouth brushed lightly over hers. Teasing, tempting. Oh, so very tempting. "That wasn't so hard," he asked. "Was it?"

She shook her head and shivered when his fingers trailed a path along the edge of the robe where it lay against her neck. "Now for the tough part," he said.

She wondered if he could hear her heart hammering against her ribs. "What's that?"

"The timing, sweetheart." He nibbled her earlobe, sending liquid fire rippling through her system.

"Oh." She sighed. "Yes. *That.*"

"I think it's time for the hero to appear on the scene."

She tipped her head to the side and nearly moaned with pleasure when he nuzzled the sensitive spot behind her ear. "Did you have a specific hero in mind?"

He planted a row of downy kisses along her jaw. "Probably a writer. They're very creative, you know."

"Mmm-hmm."

"Someone tall. And dark. He could be of Italian descent."

One long, tanned finger slipped beneath the lapel of her robe to skim over the swell of her breast. Her breath caught at the delicious intimacy. "Could be."

"I think he enjoys kissing the heroine in the backyards of palaces. Or on messy hardwood floors—he isn't choosy."

She smiled and pressed a kiss to the base of his neck. His pulse throbbed beneath her lips, strong and steady. "What do you think the hero will discover before the curtain closes?"

He pulled her into his arms. "He's hoping he'll find the answers to all his questions, and the fulfill-ment of his dreams."

"Sounds like heaven."

"He thinks it just might be," Nick murmured, and then he covered her mouth with his, demanding, tor-menting, retreating. "The hero waits for the heroine's invitation. She takes his hand, knowing where each step is leading, and shows him the way."

Sydney followed his stage directions, her pulse drumming with desire, her nerves taut with anticipa-tion. She pulled him toward the bed but hesitated near their destination.

He shifted to face her and his fingers glided along the folds of her robe, tracing her shape. "The hero has watched her for weeks, watching her body move beneath her clothes, catching the curve of a breast or the hint of a long, slender thigh. He's suddenly im-patient to put his hands on skin he's imagined touching."

The rumbling caress of his voice enthralled her, stroking her with each syllable. An air-conditioned draft moved over her as he opened her robe, but it did little to cool her fevered skin.

He took her hands and guided them until they hovered inches from his chest. "He wants her to touch him, to feel his heart pound and know it's beating for her." He dropped his hands, leaving hers so close to him. "Touch me, Sydney."

She slowly slid her hands along his chest, exploring the wide solid shape of him, and he groaned as her fingers spread over the firm swells of his muscles and slipped through the coarse, springy hair. When he shuddered beneath her touch, she lifted her face to meet his gaze and shifted to close the narrow, charged gap between them.

She hesitated, waiting for her cue and his seductive direction. He paused, drawing out the anticipation and the drugging tension.

"Kiss me, Sydney."

She moved to him with all the mindless passion his words had built inside her, and he crushed his mouth over hers in a greedy, ferocious assault. Hot and wild and desperate and glorious—and not enough. Not nearly enough. She clawed at his back, and he scraped his hands along her shoulders, stripping the robe from her and letting it fall in a thick, blue pool at her feet. At last their embrace was skin to skin—and still not enough.

"The hero wants to know all of his heroine," said Nick, his voice hoarse with strain, "to see, touch, taste every inch of her. He needs to know if she's on fire, too."

"Yes, yes, she is. I am." Sydney struggled to pull free of the tormenting fantasy and pressed against him. "Nick, please…I want…"

"Tell me, Sydney." He took her face in trembling hands. "Tell me. I'll do anything."

"What you said." Her words escaped with a quiet groan. "What you said you were going to do."

He swept her off her feet and into his arms, and his strength sent a giddy flutter through her. "Mmm. That's going to take a long time. How long before you have to go back?"

"I don't have to go back. Leave, I mean. Not now. Not later. Not really."

He smiled and lowered her, gently, sweetly, to the bed and knelt on the mattress, his gaze exploring every inch of her length. "You're so beautiful."

She lifted a hand to his face and traced the corner of his lip. He raised a large, tanned hand to curl around hers, and then slowly brought it to his lips and pressed them, long and hard, into her open palm. "The last time I did this," he murmured against her fingers, "I wanted to pull you close and never let you go." He stared at her intently. "I still feel the same way."

"*Nick.*" Her eyes pricked with tears, and she swallowed them back. "Oh, Nick."

"I don't need to pretend anymore, Sydney. I know exactly what I'm doing." He untied the towel from his waist and let it slip to the floor. "And why."

He gathered her in a lover's embrace. His mouth was insistent, his caresses like embers along her skin. She floated in a sea of sensations, each seeming more exquisite than the last. She imagined she could feel his pulse pounding its rhythm through her body, his quivering responses echoing her tremors.

He was poised above her now, beckoning to her

with the cessation of his movement. "Sydney. I want you. I want you to belong to me." Her eyes fluttered open and she saw a reflection of her own exquisite torture, her own suffocating need. "Do you understand?"

"Yes," she whispered. And then he lowered himself to her, and slipped inside her to claim her body as he had already claimed her heart.

As IF FROM a great distance, Sydney floated back to reality. Nick's breath washed across her throat in moist, intimate waves. Carefully, so not to break the spell, she lifted one hand to touch the midnight-black hair curling just beneath her chin. She marveled at its silky feel and smiled at the slight dampness.

He shifted them to their sides, cradling her back against him. Feathery kisses on her nape sent a tingling static down her spine, and she wriggled against the current.

"What are you thinking?" he asked.

"I'm hungry."

"There's just no keeping you satisfied." Nick edged up on one elbow. "What did you order, anyway?"

"Hamburgers." She slipped from his bed and into the oversize blue robe, and then she opened the door to find the room service tray in the hall. "Guess we didn't hear the knock."

He grinned. "Guess not."

"Where do you want to eat?"

Nick sat and patted the space beside him, temptation in flesh and blood. Her tousled, handsome lover.

She set the tray on the mattress and overturned one of the glasses when she climbed in beside him. "Oops. Sorry."

He brushed ice cubes to the floor and blotted the rest of the mess with a corner of the sheet. "A walking disaster," he muttered. "I'll call for maid service when we leave."

"Are we leaving?" she asked around a mouthful of hamburger.

He shot her a glance. "I don't know. Are we?"

She ran a fingertip over a dark, masculine nipple, and he lifted one dark brow. And then he took the burger from her hand, tossed it on the tray and pressed her back against the mattress.

CHAPTER TWENTY-ONE

HARLEY STOOD at her front window, staring at Norma's house. She'd popped a video in the player to keep her company on one of her rare evenings off and prepared a pot of coffee to help her stay awake through the final credits, but the comings and goings across the street were just as entertaining. More than the usual number of people had made the trip up and down the narrow stairs leading to Syd's cozy attic apartment. At the moment, Syd herself wasn't home. She'd driven off with a mysterious male visitor. Hours and hours ago.

Maybe the man was a member of the cast from the community theater where she was rehearsing a play, and he'd stopped by to offer her a lift. Maybe he was a relative who'd come by for a visit and to check out the sights. Maybe…

Harley was out of maybes. Besides, whoever he was, he hadn't looked like any of the maybes she'd thought of so far.

And wasn't that strange, because according to Norma, Sydney had finally given Hank an answer to his proposal.

The one he deserved, in Harley's opinion. An answer that left him in the same kind of limbo he'd kept her dangling in for the past few days.

Okay, so it was spiteful of her to think it, and he'd never admit to doing it, but he'd done it, just the same. No man who was serious about marrying one woman made the kind of moves he'd made, the kind of talk he'd made, with another. Especially a man like Hank.

And while she was standing there, her coffee mug in hand and maybes on her mind, Hank pulled up in his car and parked it right behind Sydney's. He jogged up her stairs, knocked on her silly blue door and waited. And waited.

And then he walked down the stairs, shoved his hands into his pockets and headed Harley's way.

Oh, no. Not again.

Whatever was going on over at Sydney's place, it didn't seem right for Hank to end up here at hers. He was either looking for Sydney, or he was looking for some more sympathy.

Second place and a shoulder to whine on. She was getting tired of settling for such a limited pair of options where Hank was concerned. She rubbed the mug over her aching heart, let the curtain fall from her hand and walked down her narrow entry hall to open her front door.

"Evenin', Hank."

"Harley." He nodded and waited. And then he cleared his throat and waited some more. "Won't you invite me in?"

"I'm not sure I want to." She set the mug on her entry table and crossed her arms over her chest. "Won't that bother your fiancée? Or, should I say, your not-quite-one-hundred-percent fiancée?"

He closed his eyes on a sigh. "You know about the engagement."

"We share everything in this neighborhood. We take Mr. Rogers seriously here."

"Sydney?"

"Norma."

"That was fast."

"That little old lady is light on her feet when she's got gossip to share." Harley leaned her shoulder against her doorjamb. "What I'm trying to figure out is the percentages involved here. If she's not one hundred percent convinced she should marry you, what is it? Fifty percent? Seventy-five?"

He narrowed his eyes. "Are we going to have the rest of this conversation on your doorstep?"

"I repeat, won't it bother your fiancée if I let you in?"

"No."

"I see. She doesn't know about what happened between us."

"There is no 'us,' Harley."

Oh, that last remark stabbed deep. Quick, and light, and with such a such a fine, sharp blade the blood was already neatly drying over the wound. There probably wouldn't even be a scar.

She wouldn't let it happen—she didn't intend to

let him leave a mark on her. "You're right about that, Hank. Good night."

She started to give the door a satisfactory shove at his face, but he threw up a hand to stop it. "Let me in, Harley."

"I don't think so."

"I want to talk to you."

"Well, I don't want to talk to you," she said, wincing at the pitiful tone of her voice.

"You don't have to say anything."

"Isn't that convenient."

He sighed and stared at his shoes. "I'm sorry you've already heard my news. I wanted to tell you myself."

"Is that why you're here?"

"Yes." He lifted his eyes to her face. "Mostly."

He looked so miserable she didn't have the heart to keep him out. She glanced across the street at Sydney's dark windows. Maybe he'd had more trouble with this, had suffered through all of this mess more than she had herself.

"Oh, all right," she said, moving to one side. "Come in."

He stepped into her cramped entry and waited for her to close the door. She waved him toward the back of her house. "You know where the kitchen is."

"Is that the best place to talk?"

"It is if you want a drink while you're doing it."

He shook his head. "I don't think that would be smart. I need a clear head for this."

"Sounds serious."

"Everything seems that way, lately."

He seemed larger than life in the narrow space, towering over her in his conservative gray suit and his conservative gray striped tie. His cologne tickled her nose and danced along her memory cells and made her toes curl. She was sure she'd always think of him whenever she smelled that particular scent on another man. But it wouldn't be quite the same scent, because it wouldn't be the same man wearing it.

The sense of loss was overwhelming, amplified by his presence and purpose in her home. So close, and yet so completely out of reach. But then, he'd always been out of reach. He'd always been Sydney's, whether she deserved him or not.

He stepped toward her, and she tilted her head back to look at him. "What is it that's so serious?" she asked.

"My life. My plans." He frowned. "My job."

"Something's wrong at work?"

"Not exactly. It's just that the partners and their wives are very, very pleased about my engagement to Sydney. My upcoming engagement, that is." He studied her intently, as if he were looking for the secret answer to some unspoken question in her eyes. "In fact, they're all a lot more pleased about it than I am."

Harley's heart flipped a foolish flip. "I thought you wanted to marry her."

"So did I."

Harley shook her head. "You've been trying to talk her into it for months now."

He nodded, still solemn, still staring, still strangely intense. "I know."

"And you finally did. Talk her into it. Sort of."

"Yes, I did."

"So why aren't you pleased she said 'maybe'?"

His lips quirked in a hint of a smile. "Because I changed my mind."

"About getting married?"

"No."

"About Sydney?"

He shook his head. "Not exactly."

"I don't understand."

"Neither do I." He reached out and gently wrapped his long fingers around her arms. "That's the other reason I'm here."

Her heart was flipping so fast now she was afraid he'd feel her vibrating. "I don't want you to kiss me."

"I don't want to kiss you, either." He slowly lowered his head, until his lips hovered a fraction of an inch over hers. "But I can't seem to help it, Harley."

His lips brushed hers, so softly, so tenderly, so bittersweet, that her heart flopped over one last time and melted into a warm lump just waiting for him to mold it into whatever shape he chose. "I can't help it, either, Hank."

He smiled and took her hand as he led her toward the back of her house. "I like it when you call me that."

"You do?"

"Yes," he said. He paused at her kitchen door. "There are all sorts of things about you that I like."

"There are?"

He nodded and widened his wonderful, handsome smile. "I like you, Harley. Very much."

Like. It was a long way from love, but she was too far gone to let it worry her now. She'd take the few crumbs he cast her way and treasure them like gold nuggets. She'd had a lot of practice at it.

She tugged at his hand and guided him down the short hall to her bedroom door. "I like you, too, Hank."

"I don't know why. We're complete opposites. We have almost nothing in common."

The utter confusion in his voice and on his face delighted her. She laughed and tossed her arms around his neck. "Oh, Hank, haven't you ever heard that opposites attract?"

"That's just a saying."

She moved in close and pressed her body along his. "Does this feel like some worn-out line?"

"No." His eyes darkened with desire. "This feels like trouble."

She loosened his tie. "Because you're still technically nearly engaged?"

"No."

"Then why?"

"Because I think I might still be nearly engaged to the wrong woman." He lifted her and carried her to her bed. "And I don't want to think about how in the hell I'm going to get myself out of this mess."

CHAPTER TWENTY-TWO

THAT TRILLING sound did not belong in this particular scene, Sydney thought as she tugged her bedspread over her head. The spread felt funny—synthetic and slippery. This wasn't her pastel crazy quilt. Her eyes flew open, blinking away a sticky film, trying to focus on the wall on the other side of the room. Sunlight illuminated a chrome-framed print hanging on green-striped wallpaper—not the antique fireplace mantel she'd used to frame a bookcase and her yellow-and-gold ragged bedroom wall. This wasn't her house.

This was Nick's hotel room. And, from the looks of it, this was morning. She rolled her head on the pillow and stared at the digital readout on the alarm radio. Early morning.

Nick knelt beside her and wrapped her fingers around her cell phone. "It's your mother," he whispered. "Your phone looks like mine, and I picked it up without thinking." He guided the phone to her ear, and then brushed a sweet, silent kiss across her lips.

"Mother," she croaked.

"Some man answered your phone." Meredith's

sigh was longer and deeper than usual. "It wasn't Henry."

Sydney rubbed her eyes and scooted upright on the bed. "Uh…"

Nick turned away from her, stretching. The muscles of his back shifted beneath his dark skin, and his jeans emphasized the lean length of his legs as he walked to his desk to frown at his laptop. Dark stubble along his jaw added a dangerous look to his rugged features. She shivered, unnerved at finding such a shady, brooding, beautiful creature sharing her room so early in the day.

"Sydney?"

"Yes." She cleared her throat.

"What is a man doing at your house at this time of day?"

Nick slipped back into his chair at the desk and tapped rapidly at his laptop keys. She'd left her phone on the desk yesterday, and he must have been working when it rang.

She darted another glance at the bedside alarm clock. Eight-thirty. "We're, uh, going out to breakfast. Together."

"And where were you last night? I phoned you several times before I left. And again when I got home."

"I must have turned off my cell." She pulled it from her ear and shook it. No stray drops. "Sorry."

"Henry was looking for you, too. He called to ask if I'd heard from you."

"Henry?"

"Yes. Henry." Her mother sighed again. "The man who wants to marry you."

Sydney winced. "I'm sorry I didn't check in."

"Never mind about that now. I called because I want to know what you'd like me to pick up for the party."

The party." Sydney swung her legs to the floor. "Mother, you don't need to—"

"Nonsense. I don't mind, and it'll be fun. I want to talk with you again today, Sydney, and this party sounds like an excellent opportunity—at least I'll know where to find you."

Sydney gave in and told her mother what time to meet at the school, disconnected with an exhausted sigh and set the phone on the bedside table. "Well, that went surprisingly well."

Nick poured a cup of coffee and handed it to her. "Here," he said. "You look like you could use this."

She winced and blinked up at him. "I do?"

"Yes. You also look all rumpled and rosy and ready for some good-morning sex."

"That's a much nicer thing to say."

He sat beside her and gently shoved the coffee toward her mouth. "Drink," he ordered.

"Yes, Mother." She took a sip. "You know how parents can be sometimes. Suffocating you for your own good."

She glanced at Nick. "Are yours like that?"

"No. We tied them to a tree once and threatened to set them on fire, and they've been pretty easy to handle since then."

She laughed and set the cup aside, and then she pulled him close to show her appreciation for the way he'd brightened her morning.

SYDNEY'S CELL PHONE rang again while she was in the shower. He checked the screen—Gracie. He figured Sydney wouldn't mind him saying hello, as long as he kept the secret of her location. "Sydney Gordon's residence."

"Like hell it is," said a female voice.

"Gracie?"

"Who the hell is this?"

"It's Nick."

Gracie laughed so loud he had to pull the receiver away from his ear. "Where are you, Nick?"

"With Sydney."

"Yes, that would explain why you've got her phone. But where are you?"

"Where are you?" He didn't want to let Gracie know Sydney was in his hotel room. Not yet.

"I asked first."

"Damn."

"I'm standing in Sydney's driveway," she said, "so I know you two aren't at her place."

"Double damn." He scrubbed a hand over his face. "We're at my place."

"Which is…?"

"Here. Near the lake."

A long silence ended with Gracie's low chuckle. "Well, well, well. Looks like our Sydney has herself quite a confusing mess on her hands. I wish I could have been there when she first saw you and realized she'd have to deal with you here, at home."

She paused, and he could hear the crackle of a gum wrapper. "So," she said, "have you battered down the castle door? Or are you still in the siege phase of this relationship?"

Sydney appeared in the bathroom doorway, her hair in curling disarray around a face flushed with heat and sleep and the aftereffects of another bout of lovemaking. Her oversize cotton shirt hung crookedly, exposing a teasing glimpse of smooth shoulder and bra strap. He cursed her preference for loose, floaty clothing. It was sexy as hell.

He dragged his attention back to Gracie's last question. "A little of both, I think."

"Well, is she there?"

"Sydney?" He glanced at her, and she frowned and reached for the phone.

"Yes, she's here. Bye, Gracie."

"Wait! Nick—"

He stood and held up a hand, signaling for more time. "Yes?"

"We're having a little get-together this afternoon," said Gracie. "All the kids who went on the Europe trip are going to be there. Why don't you come along as my date?"

"I don't know." He glanced at Sydney's murderous expression. "Life is pretty complicated right now. It's probably not a good idea."

"Au contraire, Nick," Gracie drawled in an atrocious French accent. "A little complicated is exactly what the doctor ordered."

"Is this another theory, Gracie?"

"No. A hunch."

"Even worse."

"Give me your number, and I'll call you with the details."

Nick did as she'd asked and then handed Sydney's phone to her with a shrug.

She turned away to discuss some last-minute details with Gracie, pacing across the room, and he tried to focus again on his work. This new story idea—a mysterious murder aboard a sailing yacht—was coming at him so fast he could scarcely keep up.

Sydney set the phone on the desk beside him. "What was that all about?"

"Gracie wants to visit." He turned and tugged her into his lap. "Good morning. Again."

"Good morning," she said, blushing. "How's it going?"

He reached around her, hit a key and the screen went blank. "It's not."

She straightened. "It's not?"

He nuzzled her neck. "I can't get anything done when you're here in my room, looking like an engraved invitation to a morning in paradise."

She tugged at the drooping neckline of her shirt. "Sorry, I didn't mean to disturb your work."

She tried to step away, but he caught her about the waist before she could make her escape. "Want to show me how sorry you are?"

She smiled and leaned against him. "Have something in mind, do you?"

"Yeah." He slid one hand beneath the hem of her shirt. "Research."

"What?"

"Research." He worked her collar to one side and nipped at the base of her neck. "I think my editor's going to be shocked to find a graphic love scene in the next Jack Brogan mystery."

"Might be an improvement."

He unfastened a button. "You're not going to turn critic on me again, are you?"

She slid her hands around his shoulders. "That depends."

"On what?"

"On how good you are at what you do."

"On second thought," he said as he flicked open the catch on her bra, "go ahead and disturb the hell out of me."

NICK DROPPED Sydney at her place an hour later and then headed across the river for a bite to eat. He planned to take a bit of a break from the writing, maybe kill some time checking out a construction site he'd discovered near the state park, but his phone rang as he was climbing into his car. Gracie again, and this time she wasn't taking no for an answer. What the heck—he wouldn't mind seeing the students again.

He pulled into Gracie's driveway a couple of

hours later and helped her carry party supplies to his car.

"The kids are going to be so surprised," she said as she handed him two plastic containers of punch. "They sure enjoyed hanging out with you on the tour."

"I just hope Syd doesn't mind."

Gracie lowered her box of supplies into the trunk. "Yeah, well, she may have a bit of a temper, but she cools off fast enough."

"I've seen her temper, up close and personal. Never knew anyone who could get so worked up so fast—and I grew up in an Italian family."

"Sounds like she'll fit right in."

He closed the trunk lid and grinned at her. "What are you up to? Are you matchmaking, Gracie Drew?"

"Are you looking for some?"

He shook his head and moved to the driver's side of the car. "I think I can handle it on my own."

"Hmm." Gracie climbed into the passenger side and buckled her seat belt. "You know, I've been wondering why you answered the phone this morning, and not Sydney."

Nick glanced past her, looking for an opening in the traffic that seemed to perpetually clog the lakefront. "I was closer to the phone."

"Seems a hotel room isn't all that vast. Seems she would have been able to get to it herself."

"She was busy."

"She was sleeping. Or in the shower."

He clenched his hands around the steering wheel and kept his mouth shut.

"You're clenching," she pointed out. "Good guess."

"Not fair, Gracie."

She poked his shoulder. "All's fair in love and war, and don't you forget it."

"Am I fighting a war?"

"Are you in love?" Gracie challenged. "Or just toying with my ex-roommate's affections?"

"If there's any game-playing going on here, it's not on my part." He gave her a meaningful glance. "I did a little of that in England, enough to teach me not to try it again. I figure I lost a couple of valuable days with that 'give her some space' tactic."

"Answer the question, Nick."

"All right." He sighed. "Yes. I love her."

"Ah, then it is a war." Gracie turned to face him. "The way to get Sydney to surrender is simple. Outflank her, surround her, cut off every escape route and then just sit back and wait. She'll wander into your trap sooner than you think."

"I don't want her to marry me just because she's temporarily out of other options."

"You want to marry her?" Gracie waited for his nod, a happy smile spreading across her face. "Then don't blow it," she said. "Can't you see how this works? First, she agreed to spend some time with you. After fending off your first invitations, right?"

"More or less."

"But things in Paris were pleasant."

He shot her a grin. "Extremely."

"So you showed up here on her doorstep, ready for more of the sweet stuff. She agreed. After putting up some token resistance?"

Nick arched one eyebrow at his passenger but volunteered nothing.

"Sounds to me like you've had quite a bit of success over the last few days."

"What do you mean?"

"Where did you wake up this morning?"

"That's classified."

"That's obvious." Gracie brought one finger up to tap lightly against her lips, the bright pink nail a shock against her coral lipstick. "Hmm. Knowing Sydney like I do, I'd say it's a safe bet that the first mention anyone makes about what you're up to here will give her the first big push down the aisle."

"How so?"

"She's not a fickle woman, and she won't want anyone thinking she is."

"That's going to be a tough act."

"Why?"

"Technically she's still engaged. Sort of, anyway."

"Well, this is a fine fix." Gracie pulled out a pack of gum and peeled the wrapper. "Juicy Fruit?"

"No, thanks."

She slid the gum into her mouth. "How could she have gotten herself into this mess in the first place?"

"I like to think it's because she's loyal, and sensitive, and because I hadn't stepped back into the picture yet," said Nick. "Maybe Henry won by

default, since she thought she'd never see me again."
He downshifted and muttered a mild curse at a car
that darted into his lane. "Ever since we met, there's
been this problem with our timing. It's always just a
little off. We can't seem to get a break."

"Well, she's going to have to break it off with
Henry. For good."

"She will. She already has, at least in her own
mind. But she wants to talk to him first, to try to let
him down easy." Gracie pointed down a side street,
and he made the turn. "But you just said she's not
fickle, and if it's true she doesn't want to appear to
be, how does that add up?"

"It doesn't have to. She woke up in your bed this
morning, didn't she?"

"I didn't say that."

"You didn't have to." Gracie gave him a smug
look. "And what I said still goes. She's not fickle. If
she was with you, then that's where she wants to
be."

"I'm holding on to that thought, believe me." He
scrubbed a hand over his mouth. "Why can't she
face that fact herself?"

"She's probably taking it one moment at a time,
one day at a time, hoping things will just work themselves out. It's a learned behavior. If you met her
mother, you'd understand."

He blew out a sigh. "I have."

"What?"

"Met her mother. Meredith and I were introduced

yesterday morning. She showed up about a minute after I did."

Gracie threw her head against the seat and laughed. "Oh, poor Syd. What a morning."

"Yeah. And from what I gather, Henry had gotten to her just the night before."

"And then the next night, she's holed up in your hotel room." Gracie laughed again. "She tends to be a bit impulsive, but I've never known her to move so fast. She must be feeling absolutely breathless lately."

Hearing Gracie summarize the situation, Nick felt uneasy about putting so much pressure on Sydney. There was only so much stress a person could take. "I don't want her to get hurt."

Gracie flapped a hand. "She'll land on her feet. She always does."

She gave him another direction as they neared the school buildings. "Enjoy the skirmishes. Enjoy the spoils of battle. You know, it's hard to drum up sympathy for a guy who's got everything going for him, including the affection of a beautiful, intelligent, talented woman."

"Yeah." His face eased into a wide grin as he remembered why he was putting himself through all this. "I just need to regroup. After all," he noted as he maneuvered the car across an intersection and into the school lot, "the siege is over. I have managed to batter down the castle door. So to speak."

Gracie pointed to a parking spot and rubbed her hands together. "Time to begin the treaty negotiations."

Nick turned off the engine and settled back against his seat, pinning Gracie in hers with his steeliest stare. "Listen, Gracie. I know you have our best interests at heart, and I appreciate your words of wisdom. But I took your advice once before, and it didn't work out quite the way you intended. If Sydney needs more time to decide what's right for her, then I just need the patience to let her have it. So I'm asking you to be on your best behavior this afternoon. And to stay out of the way, if you know what I mean."

"I know exactly what you mean, even if you don't," she said.

"Gracie."

"Don't worry," she said with an innocent smile. "I won't say a word to Sydney."

CHAPTER TWENTY-THREE

SYDNEY ROLLED her eyes as her mother adjusted the cookies on a plate one of the students' parents had just added to the snack table. "Mother, please. I think those were fine the way they were."

"I don't mind helping. Really." Meredith frowned as one of the students took a napkin, and then she rearranged the fanned design. "You just concentrate on your hostessing duties and I'll take care of keeping the punch bowl full."

Sydney glanced around the library conference room, watching students and parents chat over the collection of photos and souvenirs. She had to admit her mother's idea for this party had been an excellent one. And she'd like nothing better than to share memories with her students and visit with their parents. But someone had to stand guard over Meredith standing guard over the refreshments. Maybe Gracie could take a shift when she arrived.

Where was she, anyway?

"Nick!"

"Hey, Nick's here!"

The students mobbed him before he'd made it

through the door. Gracie shoved past the crowd, balancing a shopping bag and a bakery box. "Sorry we're late," she said when she arrived at the table.

"What is he doing here?" asked Sydney.

"What do you mean?"

"He wasn't invited."

"Oh, dear." Meredith sighed and stared at Nick, who stood across the room, pumping Mr. Tanner's hand after an introduction. "I suppose I should have expected something like this."

"He most certainly was invited." Gracie set her things on the table. "I invited him."

"Why would you do a thing like that?" Sydney asked. "If I'd wanted him here, I would have asked him myself."

"He was on the tour, wasn't he?" Gracie opened the box and dumped cookies on an empty plate. "And just look how excited the kids are to see him."

"You should be mingling, dear." Meredith gave Sydney a pointed look as she rearranged Gracie's cookies in a fancy spiral. "I can handle things here."

Gracie rolled her eyes behind Meredith's back. Sydney glanced across the room just in time to catch Nick wink at her over Lori's head. "All right. Maybe I will."

She made her way to one of the display tables, stopping to admire Macie's scrapbook and chat with Eric's mother, Susan Wittenauer. "Eric was full of Nick stories when he got home," said Susan. "Nick said this, Nick said that. Nick took us here and there.

I can hardly wait to meet him and thank him for showing Eric such a good time."

Sydney pasted on a polite smile. "He certainly added a lot to the experience."

Susan leaned in close and lowered her voice. "He certainly added a lot to yours, from what I heard."

Sydney's smile wavered. She muttered something about needing to check on the video presentation and moved on to look at another display.

"Hello, Ms. Gordon."

Sydney turned to find Macie's father smiling at her. "Hello, Mr. Childers."

"Please, call me Tom."

"Tom." Sydney extended her hand. "Macie's a wonderful young lady. I'm so glad I got to spend some quality time with her this summer."

"Thank you. Yeah, she's a great kid. And she's so excited she got the chance to introduce me to Nick. We've been hearing a lot about him. You're a lucky lady."

"I am?"

"Macie said you two hit it off in Paris. Things must be getting serious if he cut his trip short to come back and spend the rest of his vacation with you."

"Macie told you that?"

"No, Nick did."

Sydney's left eye started twitching. "He did, did he?"

"Macie thinks it's great. I do, too. He seems like a real nice fellow."

"Thank you, Mr.—Tom."

"And thank you for taking such good care of my girl."

Sydney turned, located Nick and headed in his direction. Matt's mother cut her off. "Sydney! Omigosh, I can't believe *Nick Martelli* is here."

"Neither can I."

"Matt could hardly wait to introduce me. He knows what a fan I am."

Nick was a charming guy, and Matt's mother was a bit of a flake, but this was carrying things a bit too far. "A fan?"

"Of his show. I've taped every one."

"His show?"

"Don't tell me you've never seen *Building on History?* Omigosh, it's the coolest building show on cable."

Sydney's stomach hit the floor and rebounded to lodge in her throat. "No. I've never seen it."

"It's usually on early Saturday mornings—worth getting up for. They take these interesting old buildings—I don't know where they find them—last week it was a chapel, and the stained glass was fabulous—and they turn them into these incredible one-of-a-kind houses. It's absolutely *amazing* what they can do with them."

"I'm sure it is." *Specialty construction. Architectural salvage.* Had some money saved up and handed his "business" over to his assistant for a while, hmm? No mysteries about Nick Martelli, hmm?

She curled her fingers into fists and clenched them tight.

"But the best part of the show is watching *him*." Matt's mother looked over her shoulder with a sigh. "I thought he was hot with the tool belt and all, but in person—*omigosh*."

"Excuse me." Gracie tapped Sydney on the arm. "Henry's here."

"What?"

"Henry." She pointed behind Sydney. "Is here."

Sydney groaned. "What next?"

"Sydney?"

She groaned again and turned to face her mother. "Yes?"

"Your fiancé would like to talk to you."

"Your fiancé?" Matt glanced up from a display table. "You're engaged? To Nick?"

"No," said Meredith. "To Henry Barlow. Why would you think she's engaged to Nick?"

"Because she was always kissing him and stuff when we were in France," said Matt. "Who's Henry?"

"He is," said Gracie, pointing to where Henry stood, looking strained and stiff and straightening his tie near the snack table. "He's Mr. Barlow. He and Ms. Gordon got engaged yesterday. Well, sort of engaged."

"Actually it was the day before," said Meredith. She shot a dark glance in Nick's direction. "Sydney, may I speak with you?"

"Not now, Mother." Sydney started across the

room to find out why Henry had decided to make an appearance at the party. Then again, why not? Everyone else was crashing the place as if it were the hottest nightclub in New York.

"Sydney," said Henry as she approached. "We've got to talk."

"This is a really bad time, Henry."

"I can see that, and I'm sorry. It's just that—"

"Ms. Gordon?"

Sydney gritted her teeth to keep her smile in place and turned to face Eric. "Yes?"

"Did you break up with Nick or something?"

"Eric," she said, "I'd like you to meet Henry Barlow. My fiancé."

"How do you do," said Henry as he held out his hand.

"How do you do," said Eric as he shook it. His face was bright red. "I just wanted some punch. That's all."

"Here, let me get that for you," said Henry. He picked up the ladle, dribbled some red juice into a plastic cup and handed it to Eric. "I've been hearing a lot about Nick ever since I got here. How did you meet him, anyway?"

"Not now, Henry. This isn't a good time." Sydney turned and scanned the room, looking frantically for a large display table or a potted palm or an oil tanker to duck behind, and instead she saw Norma and Harley Maxwell walk into the room. *"Not now."*

"Sydney!" Norma called out with a neighborly wave. "I brought some cookies."

"Oh, my God," Henry moaned from behind Sydney. "What is she doing here?"

"Norma?" asked Sydney. "She brought cookies."

"Not Norma. *Harley.*"

The way he said her name made Sydney turn and study his face. It looked a little pale. "Henry?"

"Not now, Sydney," he said. "This isn't a good time."

She turned to find Matt and Macie glaring at her. "Would you like some punch?" she asked.

"Sure." Macie held out a plastic cup. "What's with that guy?"

"Which one?" Sydney asked, feeling a little queasy.

"Him," said Matt, pointing to Henry.

"He's Henry Barlow," said Sydney. "And we're engaged."

"I told you so," Matt said to Macie.

"But, Ms. Gordon," said Macie with a sorrowful look. "What happened to you and Nick?"

"Sydney?" Meredith approached the table. "You should be mingling."

Sydney closed her eyes. The twitch was getting so bad she was afraid it would spread. Any moment she might fall to the floor in a full body version.

"Ms. Gordon?"

She opened her eyes to see Eric's mother, Susan, standing next to Norma at the other end of the snack table. "Eric just told me the good news. Congratulations on your engagement!"

"Which one?" asked Norma.

"I—" Susan's smile faded. She looked confused. "I don't know what you mean. Which engagement?"

"No," said Norma as she bit into a cookie. "Which man?"

Susan sputtered with an embarrassed little laugh, and then she stared at Sydney and Meredith. "Excuse me," she said. "I think I'll go take another look at the displays."

Harley walked toward the table, dressed in her casino uniform.

"Hi, Harley," said Sydney. "Boy, am I glad to see a friendly face."

"Oh, *Sydney*," she said and burst into tears.

"Harley!" Henry shifted past Sydney and pulled Harley into his arms. "What happened?"

"Sydney said something to her," said Norma.

"What did you say?" Henry looked furious. "How could you be so cruel?"

"All I said was 'hi.'" Sydney narrowed her eyes at her neighbor. Harley was a terrible actress, though the tears were impressive.

"She's probably just feeling guilty," said Norma, and took another cookie. "Because Henry spent the night at her house last night."

Sydney shifted her gaze to Henry. It wasn't just her imagination. He was definitely pale. And a little green around the edges. Harley buried her face in his jacket.

"Henry!" Meredith placed a hand on Sydney's arm. "Is it true?"

"We're going to leave now," said Susan, with a

glance in Harley's direction. "Thank you for a lovely time."

"Thank you for coming," said Sydney. *Take me with you.*

A hush had fallen over the room—except for Harley's sobs. Students and their parents gathered their things and made quick farewells to Gracie, practically stumbling over each other in their hurry to escape.

Nick wandered over to the table. "Finally a break. I thought I'd never get a cookie."

"Take one of the almond ones," said Norma. "They're great."

"Don't mind if I do." He stuck out his hand. "I'm Nick."

"I figured," she said.

Nick grinned at Sydney. "That went pretty well, don't you think?" he asked. "Great idea for a party. Everyone had a nice time."

Everyone stared at him.

He turned to Meredith. "Hello, Mrs. Gordon."

Meredith looked as if she were considering other options than responding politely. "Hello."

"Well, that wrapped up earlier than expected," said Gracie as she joined them at the table. "Let's clear this stuff up and then we can head for home."

"I'll help," said Sydney.

Nick's grin took on a wicked edge as he turned toward Henry. "Don't believe we've met," he said and thrust out his hand. "Nick Martelli."

"Henry Barlow."

"Pleased to meet you, Henry."

"I find that hard to believe," said Meredith under her breath.

"Me, too," said Norma as she reached for another cookie. "Considering that Sydney took off with him yesterday afternoon. And she didn't come back all night."

Harley lifted her head from Henry's damp suit jacket. "What was that?"

Gracie leaned in close to Sydney. "I've always liked that Norma," she whispered in her ear. "Calls 'em like she sees 'em."

"Shut up, Gracie," said Sydney.

"Okey-dokey, then," said Gracie. "I think I'll just empty this punch bowl."

"Here," said Nick. "Let me help you with that."

"I think you've already done quite enough here," said Meredith as she moved to take charge of the punch. "Thank you."

"No trouble," said Nick. His fingers curled over the sides of the bowl. "Besides," he said with a wink for Sydney, "it's the chivalrous thing to do."

"No." Sydney shot him a panicked look. "Not now."

"Sydney?" asked Henry.

"Oh, *Hank*," said Harley with a loud sniff.

"You're right," he said. "Not now." He led Harley to another corner of the room.

"I'll help Gracie in the kitchen," said Norma. "Maybe I could take some of these cookies for my bridge group."

"Knock yourself out," said Sydney. *And hit me with the same club.*

She looked at Henry and Harley cuddling in the corner, and she listened to her mother and Nick arguing over kitchen chores, and she heard Gracie and Norma having a rollicking good time reliving the party highlights. *Oh dear oh dear oh...* Damn.

She put her fingers in her mouth and whistled.

The conversations stopped. Gracie and Norma came to the kitchen door. Everyone stared at her.

"I'll clean this up," Sydney said. "All by myself. I don't need any help. I want you all to leave. *Right now.*"

"But Syd—" said Gracie.

"Sydney!" said Meredith.

"Out!" said Sydney. "Out, out, *out*! All of you! Right now!"

"Time to go," said Nick, pulling his car keys out of his pocket. "I've seen her when she gets like this. It isn't pretty."

"I'll call you—" said Henry.

"Out!"

"Sydney," said Meredith. "I really must insist—"

"You, too, Mother." Sydney pointed to the door. "Especially you."

"Come on, Meredith," said Norma. "I've got the almond cookies. We can move the party to my place."

CHAPTER TWENTY-FOUR

"For cryin' out loud."

Henry pulled to the side of the road a couple of miles from the school, turned off the engine, yanked the key out of the ignition and turned to glare at Harley. "When you turn on the tears, you really turn them on."

"Syd's not the only actress in town." Harley swiped at her face and smiled at him. "Got you out of there, didn't it?"

"I might have thought of something a little more…"

"Dignified?"

"I can be pretty good at diplomacy, you know."

Harley unbuckled her seat belt, scooted closer to him, tossed her arms around his neck and nibbled on his earlobe. "There's a whole bunch of things you're pretty good at, Hank."

"Yeah?"

"Yeah."

He frowned. "But there's one thing I'm lousy at."

"What's that?"

"Being engaged."

"Oh." She loosened her grip on him and sank back into her own seat. "Yeah, you pretty much stink at that."

He tapped his fingers against the steering wheel. "Makes me a little hesitant to try it again."

Harley felt another batch of tears coming on. Genuine ones this time. She sank lower in her seat and stared out the windshield. "I can see your point."

"I can think of one solution to the problem." He tightened his grip on the wheel. "Skip the engagement. Go straight to the marriage part."

"That could work."

"Strap yourself in," he said. He started the car and made a U-turn as he pulled back onto the road. "We're heading to Reno."

"We are?"

He shot her a quick, intense look, the kind of look that made her heart flip and flop. She loved it when he looked at her that way. "We're eloping," he said. "Whether you want to or not."

She buckled her belt. "If this is an example of your skill with diplomacy, I've got some bad news for you, Hank."

"I'll get you a ring later. After I propose. After the honeymoon."

"Aren't some of those things in the wrong order?"

"Shut up, Harley. The next words I want to hear from you are *I do*."

She settled back against her seat with a satisfied smile.

"Harley?"

She didn't answer.

He slipped one hand off the steering wheel and reached toward her. She slipped her fingers through his and squeezed.

He brought her hand to his lips, brushed a kiss over her knuckles and then pressed her hand to his chest. "A woman after my own heart."

SYDNEY LOUNGED barefoot on her sofa later that afternoon, watching a black-and-white classic video and eating a dinner of cookies and ice cream. She knew she should have gone to the theater to work on the set, but she was giving herself twenty-four hours to stop feeling guilty about every little thing. Including her meal choices.

Someone knocked on her door, and though she was tempted to ignore the summons, she peeked over the back of the sofa and through the lace curtain panel. Her mother.

She'd let her come in, she decided, but she wasn't going to share the cookies. "It's open," she called.

Meredith opened the door and stepped inside. "Hello, Sydney."

"Hello, Mother. Make yourself at home." *You always do, thoroughly.*

"I came to talk to you." Meredith stared at the video. "If you don't mind."

Sydney picked up the remote and pressed a few buttons. The room darkened as the glow from the television disappeared, and she flipped the switch on the old reading lamp that curved over one sofa arm.

"I've been downstairs. At Norma's," said Meredith. She smoothed her hands over her wrinkled slacks. "Talking to Gracie."

"Gracie's a lot of fun."

"Yes, she is. I like her very much, mostly because, well…" Meredith twisted her hands together uneasily. "She thinks a great deal of you. She told me there's no doubt you'll get the teaching job you've applied for."

"I think so, too."

"That's good to hear."

"Yes. You won't have to worry about me moving back in with you when my money runs out."

"I was never worried about that. Well, I was worried about the money, but—" Meredith gestured at the sofa. "May I join you?"

Sydney moved her dinner things to the trunk and scooted to one side. Her mother settled gingerly on a plump sofa cushion and leaned against a clump of needlework pillows. "What were you watching?"

To Have and Have Not.

"Sounds appropriate."

Sydney snorted and shot a suspicious glance at her mother. It usually took a couple of drinks to get Meredith loose enough to crack a joke. Norma must have thrown quite a post-party party.

"Have you heard from Henry?" asked Meredith.

"No."

"So you haven't had a chance to speak with him yet."

"No."

"Gracie thinks a great deal of Nick, too."

It stung, like it always did, when her mother valued the opinions and judgments of other people over her own daughter's. "She doesn't know him as well as I do."

"And how well do you know him?"

"Not well at all, as it turns out."

"Well, that's what a courtship is for. To learn what you need to know about the other person."

"Nick isn't courting me."

"He flew a long way for a visit with a friend." Meredith tapped her fingers on the sofa arm. "I'm prepared to be open-minded about this…situation. And about him."

"I appreciate that, Mother. I really do." Sydney shifted to face her. "But I don't need your permission or your blessing or your open-minded attitude."

"No, you don't."

"It's my life, and I'm going to blunder my way through it my own way."

"Yes, I know." Meredith smiled sadly. "I never could stop you from making all those mistakes, you know. No matter how hard I tried to keep you from getting hurt."

Mothers. Mothers were what happened to you while you were busy making other plans. Sydney sighed and picked up one of the boxes on the trunk. "Cookie?"

SYDNEY SWORE when her phone rang that evening. She huddled deeper into the battered old quilt she liked to drape over her sofa and waited for the answering machine to kick in. She promised herself she wouldn't listen, but when she heard Henry's disembodied voice on the recorder, she raced to her dining table and snatched up the receiver. If there was anyone she needed to talk to, it was Henry. Good old, steady, serious Henry. Okay, so he wasn't as steady as she'd thought, but he deserved a little of what she'd been getting on the side.

"I'm here," she said.

"Oh." There was a long pause. "Okay, then."

"What were you saying? I didn't catch the first part of your message." Another long pause. "Henry?"

"Yeah." She could hear him take a deep breath. "The thing is, I had a talk with Nick. A long one."

She closed her eyes on a wince. "Henry, I—"

"No, let me finish. He's a good man, Sydney." She heard his low chuckle. "I have to hand it to the guy. He shows up out of nowhere, takes you away from me, and I like him in spite of it all."

"Yes." She sighed. "He has that effect on people."

"You sound like you don't approve."

"Oh, no, I do." She ran her fingers through her hair, combing curls out of her eyes. "You have to admire a talent like that."

"There must be more going on here than an appreciation for the guy's charm, Sydney. I know you. You wouldn't toss aside a marriage proposal for that."

"You're right." She bit her lip and felt her stomach

twinge with a few dregs of guilt. "And there's more to it than that."

"Yeah, I heard."

"What did you hear?"

"That you two are, and I quote, 'an item.'"

"Let me guess," she said. "Matt, right?"

"Cute kid."

"You and I were an 'item' too, Henry." She winced at her use of the past tense.

"Yes, we were. But not anymore." He paused. "You know, I don't think you ever looked at me the way you look at him."

Because I never wanted to rip you apart with my bare hands. "I'm sorry."

"Don't be," he said. "You've got nothing to be sorry for. You can't help the way you feel. Just like you can't choose the person who makes you feel that way."

"But that doesn't excuse what I did. What I've done to you."

He sighed. "You didn't do anything I haven't done to you."

"I guess that's right." She smiled. "Norma. Cute kid."

"Listen, Sydney, I can't talk much longer. I've got to go."

"But Henry, I—"

"I called to tell you that I got married tonight."

She dropped into one of the dining chairs and winced as a staple on a pamphlet stabbed her. "You what?"

"Harley and I eloped to Reno." He laughed, and she imagined him shaking his head in amazement. "I hope you'll wish us well," he said.

"I do." She laughed, too. "*Congratulations.* And all the luck in the world—not that you'll need any more of that. Harley's the luckiest woman I know."

"You're telling me. She's already ahead a couple of hundred on the slots."

"That's not what I meant, Henry." Sydney pressed her lips together and fought back a sudden rush of happy, sentimental tears. "She'll make you happy. Much happier than I ever could have."

"I know that now." He paused, and she could hear Harley's voice in the background. "I'm crazy about her, Sydney."

"That's wonderful."

"No, I mean, I'm crazy about her. As in insane. She makes me crazy. I am crazy. I can't believe I did this."

"Got married?"

"No. I wanted to get married." He sighed. "I just didn't expect to get married to someone who was named after her father's favorite motorcycle."

"It could have been worse."

"Yeah. He could have named her after his favorite beer."

Sydney had never known Henry had such a wry sense of humor. He sounded almost…almost like Nick.

And he sounded happy. So much happier than

he'd ever sounded when he'd been with her. "I think she's wonderful," said Sydney. "I always have."

"Yeah. She is. And she says the same thing about you."

"Oh," said Sydney, fighting back tears. "That's nice to hear."

"Listen, Sydney, I've gotta run."

"Okay. Tell Harley congratulations for me, okay?"

"Right. 'Night, Sydney."

He disconnected before she had time to say *Goodbye, Henry.*

NICK SAT at his hotel room window the morning after the tour party disaster, staring out at a perfect blue sky, a perfect mountain backdrop and a perfect arrangement of small sails on clear water. He was staring at it, but he wasn't seeing it. He couldn't see any further than the churning mess inside him.

Now that he'd met Henry Barlow, he could see why Sydney had been so reluctant to cut the guy loose. He was taller than Nick, and possibly more handsome on a really good day, and the kind of steady, solid, responsible man that appealed to women who were looking for respectability and security.

He was also a little stuffy. Just like Sydney had been when Nick first met her. If she wanted to keep up the uptight act, Henry was a good bet to share the stage with. He'd keep her from slipping up.

Nick knew the type. He knew Henry's world, all too well. Nick could play steady—he'd done it for years. He could be solid—he'd done it while building a reputation as a builder people could trust. He could do responsible—he'd met some horrendous deadlines under horrendous conditions.

The problem was, now that he'd done it, now that he'd reached the kinds of goals most men set for themselves, he'd discovered there were other goals that meant more to him. He wanted to stretch his mind and his imagination more than he wanted to stretch his net worth. He might not get another chance—he wasn't getting too close to forty yet, but he wasn't getting any younger, either. He didn't want to face a mid-life crisis without having chased after his dream of selling a novel. Or two or three. He didn't want to be a builder or a businessman for the rest of his life. He wanted to be a writer. He had to find out if he could pull it off.

And what was he accumulating all that net worth for, anyway? He didn't have anyone to share it with. Sure, he had nieces and nephews and friends who appreciated his willingness to invest, among other things. But the children weren't his, and more often than not the investments led to the accumulation of more net worth to give away to more nephews and nieces.

Now that he'd found Sydney, there were plenty of reasons to stay off the treadmill. They could travel—she loved it, he could tell. They could enjoy an exciting, stimulating lifestyle—he'd write, she'd act and they'd meet interesting, creative people. They could be happy with a warm, simple home—now that he'd seen her place, he knew she found pleasure in basic things.

Only problem was, if he wanted her, he might have to step right back on that treadmill to get her. He knew he wasn't the best marriage prospect in sight right now. The writing career was a risky proposition, and though he had plenty in savings, his funds would start to dwindle before too long. Sydney deserved better than a gamble—she deserved security. She deserved the best he could provide for her, and he wanted to give her anything her heart desired.

Meredith Gordon would expect no less.

Nick sighed and rubbed his hands over his face. The idea that he might have to put his dreams on hold grated on his very soul. And what made the whole idea particularly tough to take was that he'd been down this road before. He'd made these kinds of sacrifices before, for his first fiancée. He'd ended up wasting his time and his talents, and he'd ended up unmarried in the bargain.

Well, okay, the unmarried part had turned out to *be* a bargain, after all.

But this time around, the woman in question hadn't even said "yes" yet. If he did what he was thinking of doing, and Sydney turned him down, he was ten times the fool he'd been before.

He was already a fool. Here he was, sitting in a California hotel room instead of tramping through Europe on a trip he'd planned and anticipated for months. A trip that was supposed to launch his new life, a trip that was supposed to provide the inspiration for his first novel.

Must be why he was sitting here now, setting himself up to be an even bigger fool.

But oh, if he won her—what a prize. He closed his eyes and let the image of color-flecked hazel eyes, soft red-gold spirals and smiling lips drift through him, soothing him. Sydney was worth any gamble, any price.

If he was going down in flames, it might as well be a bonfire.

Joe had wanted to know if he still knew how to romance a woman, how to court her. Well, Nick Martelli was about to prove that he could put everything—his work, his dreams, his life—on the line in one huge romantic quest. He picked up the phone and dialed the number he'd been carrying around in his wallet for the past couple of days.

SYDNEY STOOD in front of her bedroom mirror twenty-four hours after the post-tour party and swore under her breath. Another stuck zipper.

She supposed she could wiggle her way out of the formfitting sundress. But she wanted to wear it. She'd bought it especially for Nick. He'd appreciate the tight bodice, spaghetti straps and short skirt. It was one way to make up for all the murderous thoughts she'd been thinking about him. Now that she'd followed her mother's advice and taken twenty-four hours to think things through, all she wanted was one good, swift kick to his shin, and then they could get back to doing what they'd been doing before things had gotten a little out of control.

Someone knocked on her front door.

She walked through her living area and peeked through the door's lace curtain and froze in amazement at what she saw: a Nick Martelli who was an image of refinement. His midnight-black three-piece suit was exquisitely tailored, accentuating his lean frame and dark features with a subtle, seductive effect. A conservatively patterned silk tie coordinated with the silver tones of the folded handkerchief in his breast pocket. Italian shoes shone beneath the sharp creases of his slacks, and the glint of a thin watch at his wrist was a rich contrast to the crisp white cuffs of his shirt. Only the small, wire-handled shopping bag he held at one side spoiled the effect of suave elegance.

She opened the door for a better look. His hair— he'd had it trimmed. His cologne was rich and woodsy and male, and the bruises had disappeared completely from his freshly shaved face. He was a *GQ* fantasy come to life.

"May I come in?" he asked politely.

His voice snapped her out of her trance. "Sorry. Yes, of course."

"Looks like you need some help fastening your dress again." He set the bag on the table behind her and gently turned her around. He maneuvered the delicate fabric of the low-backed sundress through the zipper head, and she shivered when one of his knuckles brushed her bare back. His warm breath washed over her nape as he slowly, carefully refastened the zipper, driving her mad with his teasing touch.

"I was just on my way over to see you," she said when he'd finished tormenting her. She walked to the table and picked up a paper plate wrapped in plastic. "I made you some cookies. Chocolate chip."

"They look good."

"I didn't follow the directions. I added some peanut butter at the last minute. It seemed like a good idea at the time."

One corner of his mouth twisted up in amusement. "Interesting."

"Well, we'll find out." She set the cookies next to the bag. "What's in there?"

"A gift, for old times' sake."

She resisted—barely—the temptation to peek inside. "Thank you."

"I have something to discuss with you." Nick motioned her to the sofa. "Sit down, Sydney."

"This sounds serious," she said as she sank to the sofa.

"You could say that." He started to speak again, and then pressed his lips together in a frown. He turned to stare out her window, pushing his jacket back and slipping his hands into his pants pockets. "I took a job. A construction job. I'm buying a rehab project near the lake. A little more basic than what I usually do, but I'm sure I'll make a healthy profit when I turn it over."

She straightened and fought back a little wave of panic. "I thought you wanted to write."

"I'll still write. In my spare time. I'm not giving that up." He turned to face her. "I asked a woman to marry me once before, and she gave me a list of conditions to meet. You never did that, and I'm grateful. But the conditions still exist. You need security. You want a man with a steady paycheck and a stable future. You want someone who holds a regular job and works in a respectable field. You deserve those things."

"I never said I wanted them."

"You didn't need to. But I figure that's what Henry Barlow offered you, and I figure that's a big part of why you considered marrying him."

She shook her head, fighting off some familiar lung-squeezing, temple-throbbing sensations. "Maybe that was part of it, at first. When he proposed the first time, that is. But I didn't marry him. I didn't love him, not the way I should, and I couldn't go through with it."

"Thank God."

"And anyway," she said, crossing her arms and settling back against the pillows, "solid, steady, respectable Henry eloped to Reno last night with my neighbor, the blackjack dealing cocktail waitress."

"He did?"

"Yes."

"With Harley?"

She nodded.

Nick's grin spread wide. "Way to go, Hank."

She smiled, too, but her smile faded. "Why are you here, Nick?"

"There's that question again." He dragged an unsteady hand through his hair. "Look, I know marriage is a big step. And maybe you've had more practice with the proposal part, but I've had more experience with engagements. I've also had more time to think about what comes next. Hell, I've had years to think about it. Maybe I'm not being fair to you, not giving you all the time you need."

He glanced at her with a faint grin. "You seem to need an awful lot of it."

She felt a sharp stab of guilt, remembering the night in Montmartre he'd told her the story of his previous engagement. She remembered her lack of sympathy for the woman who'd promised to love him, then kept him waiting for a commitment. She'd treated Henry poorly; she didn't want to do the same to Nick.

"Why does all this have to be so hard?" she asked. "I thought love was supposed to make two people happy."

"It can, if they let it."

He crossed the room to stand before her. "I've been thinking there's no big mystery here. Maybe we've both been throwing up barriers to happiness because we were more afraid of losing it than finding it. If you keep looking for couples who aren't happy, who don't work, you're going to keep finding them because they're out there. Trapped in their misery and hanging on to their unhappiness out of habit, for as many reasons as there are people who choose to take that road in life.

"Happiness is scary as hell, Sydney, because it's so elusive. Love is the biggest gamble around. And to stand up in front of God and dozens of people you care about and promise to stay together—not only to stay together, but to be happy and to love each other for ever and ever—well, it's got to be the craziest idea anyone ever invented."

He settled on the sofa next to her and took her hand. "Someone recently dared me to prove I can be romantic, and I ended up discovering I'm a romantic fool who thinks that saying the words in that marriage vow is the most romantic act there is. It tells the world that here are two people who aren't willing to simply gamble on their love or take their best shot at happiness. It tells the world they're going to reach out and hold on to happiness with both hands, with all the power of that love, and never let go."

He reached up and touched her cheek. "I wanted to look into your eyes and see the little white house, the kids, the dog, the chocolate chip cookies. For a while, I was worried when I couldn't find them. But now I watch your sweet face when I'm inside you, and I count all the colors in those chameleon eyes of yours. And instead of looking for the things I thought would make me happy, I'm finding happiness in the things I see. I'm fighting to hold on to that happiness with both hands, with all my strength, with everything I can bring to the battle.

"I told you that I need you, Sydney. I do. You're the key to all that happiness. Because I love you."

"You do?"

"You're still not sure?" He leaned back and frowned at her. "God, woman, I just spilled my heart out to you. I almost had myself in tears here. Is this what you used to put Henry through?"

She felt a blush creeping along her cheeks. "No."

"That's right." He stood and paced back to the window, shoving a hand through his hair again and mussing his neat trim. "You used to just tell him 'no.'"

"I thought you were glad I told him 'no.'"

"I am." He sighed and closed his eyes. "Where was I?"

"Asking me to marry you?"

"Right." He snatched the bag off the table and shoved it at her. "I don't have a ring, so I brought this instead."

"The engagement present." She fingered colorful tissue paper and ribbon streamers.

"I'm hoping it can be an engagement present. That's up to you."

"Was that the proposal?"

He narrowed his eyes. "Will you just open the damn bag?"

She frowned. "That's not very romantic."

"Sorry." He took a deep breath. "I'm a little rusty on this part."

Buried inside the layers of paper and ribbon was a simple pine frame. She pulled it out and saw an inscription on a card glued to the brown-papered back. *We'll always have Paris. Love, Nick.*

Nick, Nick, Nick. She turned the frame around and glimpsed, through rapidly blurring eyes, pastel shutters and shadows on a Montmartre street.

One tear escaped to trickle down her cheek as she looked up at him.

Though her vision was wavering, she could see the panic on his face. "I know I'm not the perfect man, Sydney, but I'm working on it. Marry me. Please."

"Oh, Nick," she whispered as she wiped her nose with the back of her hand. "You're the perfect man for me. I'm very, very sure."

He reached over the colorful mess in her lap and tilted her chin up with one knuckle to kiss the tears from her cheeks. "Is that a yes, you'll marry me yes?"

"Yes."

"Just making sure."

She lifted her arms and circled his neck. "I love you, Nick."

"I love you, too." He rested his forehead against hers. "Looks like we finally got the timing right."